CHRISTMAS BOYFRIEND

About the Author

Stephanie Webb Dillon resides in Memphis, Tennessee. She is married and has three daughters and six grandchildren. Stephanie enjoys spending time with her friends having game nights and crafting. Writing is her passion. She has completed her first book series this year and started two more. She is looking forward to traveling to book events in the next couple of years, meeting other authors, models, photographers and her readers.

You can follow her on her page at amazon.com/author/sdillon9614

Also By

Freedom Colorado Series:
Baked with Love
Playing for Keeps
Sheriff's Convenient Bride
Daddy's Second Chance
The Scars Within
Guarding her Heart

Men of Phoenix Security Series:
Hidden Desires
Uncovering her Secrets

Ripper's MC Series:
Undertaker's Match
Christmas Boyfriend
Hawk's Redemption ....to be released Jan 2024

Copyright © 2023 by Stephanie Webb Dillon

All rights reserved.

No part of this publication may be reproduced, distributed, or transmitted in any form or by any means, including photocopying, recording, or other electronic or mechanical methods, without the prior written permission of the publisher, except as permitted by U.S. copyright law. For permission requests, contact [include publisher/author contact info].

The story, all names, characters, and incidents portrayed in this production are fictitious. No identification with actual persons (living or deceased), places, buildings, and products is intended or should be inferred.

Cover artist: RLS Images, Graphics & Design/ Michelle RLS Sewell

Photographer: David Wills

Cover Model: Christopher Correia

1st edition 2023

1

Sophie

Christmas used to be my favorite time of year. I loved all the festivities, decorations, baking all of it. This year, not so much. My sister Pamela was engaged to some doctor and my parents kept asking me if I was going to be bringing anyone home for Christmas dinner. It wasn't like it was a onetime casual ask either. They were hounding me about it. I don't remember the last time I had a date. I stay busy, I work all day, volunteer at the animal shelter and then come home. I'm a shy introvert. I don't socialize much, I never have. I like animals, my cat is my main companion. I have one friend, Cara. She runs the animal shelter that I volunteer at. Cara and I grew up together and have been friends since the first grade. She has been encouraging me to find a date to take to Christmas dinner. That's hard when most people want to spend Christmas with their own family.

Crunching numbers for one of my biggest clients, I don't realize someone is standing by my desk. I hear a throat clear and look up into the prettiest brown eyes I have ever seen. Too bad they are connected to an obnoxious coworker.

2

"What do you need Mr. Wilson?" I asked him annoyed. Mostly because I'm attracted to him, and I don't want to be. I finish the tape I was running and then sit back.

"Now Ms. Boyd, no reason to be hostile, I was just wondering if you were going to be attending the Christmas party next Friday?" he asked as he stood there looking all suave and sexy. Austin Wilson was an attractive man. He was about 5'10, dark eyes, bald but with a dark beard and a beautiful olive complexion. He was lean and looked great in a shirt and tie. I also knew he was affiliated with the motorcycle club in town. I wasn't sure how. I had seen him on a bike, he rode it until the weather was so cold and icy that it would be uncomfortable.

"Ms. Boyd? Sophie?" I realized he was still talking to me. Ugh I always did this. My mind wanders and I end up looking like a fool.

"I wasn't planning on going to the party, Mr. Wilson." I mumbled as I opened another file to start working on it. He leaned against my desk and crossed his arms frowning at me.

"Mr. Heath expects all of us to be there. I'm pretty sure you have to attend to receive your Christmas bonus." He stated as he looked at me with that smug smile. UGH, why of all people did I have to be attracted to someone I don't even like. "I was actually going to see if you wanted to go with me unless you have a boyfriend you plan to bring."

My eyes shot up and I was at a loss for words. He was asking me out. I thought he hated me. He was always picking on me and making snarky comments. It must be a joke, no way he wants to have me on his arm.

"Very funny Wilson. You expect me to believe you want to take me as your date?" Shaking my head, I picked up one of the files I was working on to try and ignore him. "I have to finish this account before I leave."

He didn't say anything, so I looked up at him and he was frowning. He turned and went to his office, and I found myself watching as he left. The man filled out a pair of dress pants very nicely. Shrugging my shoulders, I went back to working on the file I had started. Christmas was two weeks away. Now I have two events I needed a date for. DAMN. The rest of the day flew by and before I knew it everyone was leaving. I closed down my computer and took my purse out of the bottom drawer of my desk. I had not seen Mr. Wilson leave yet and I wanted to get out the door before he came out of his office.

I was getting in my car when my phone rang. I pulled it out and saw it was my mother. Great, just what I need at the end of a weird day. I put her on the speaker phone and answered the call.

"Hey Mom?" I said as I started toward my apartment. "I just got off work, is everything ok?" I held my breath waiting for her to start in on me. I knew she wanted me to find someone and to be happy. I just wasn't sure how to do that. I was an introvert. I would rather curl up with a book and read than go out to a bar. My sister was the social butterfly.

"Sophie, are you going to be coming for dinner tomorrow night?" her mom asked with an annoyed tone. "Pam will have Jamie with her. It would be nice to round out the table."

"Why does that matter?" I asked as I pulled out of the parking lot and started for home. "How about I just stay home then your table will be perfect." I hung up and turned off the ringer. I really didn't want to go anyway; I mean seriously why would I want to go watch my sister and her fiancé make eyes at each other all night. I sighed as I pulled into my apartment complex and got out. I went inside and headed straight for my bedroom. LeStat followed me meowing wanting his dinner. Taking my clothes off I hopped in the shower to wash off my day. When I was finished, I threw on my comfy pajamas and grabbed a bottle of wine from the fridge and a glass. I wasn't really hungry, but I still took some cheese and crackers to the living room to eat with the wine. I went back into the kitchen and opened a can of tuna for LeStat. I turned on one of my favorite shows to watch as I drank my wine. Friday, at least I wouldn't have to deal with Austin Wilson again until Monday.

What is it with that guy that pushes my buttons? We have been working together for over a year and he always manages to grate my nerves. He is really good at his job and while he seems arrogant, he has never been overly hostile to me or anything. I can't pinpoint what it is that makes me tense up anytime he comes around me. I feel like he is always watching me. I have never liked being micromanaged. I know my job and I don't need someone standing over me to tell me to do it. I was sipping my wine when my phone rang. Glancing down I saw it was Cara.

"Hey, how are things at the shelter?" I asked her as I nibbled on some of the cheese on my plate. I heard some barking in the background. "Seriously, it's almost seven and you're still at work?"

"I know but we had a couple of dogs dropped off and I wanted to make sure they were settled in. Poor things, one of them looks like he is malnourished." she said sadly. "How are you going to deal with Christmas this year?"

"Ugh, I don't even want to think about it. Now I am not only expected to bring someone to Christmas dinner, but we have a mandatory Christmas party at work, and I have to find a date for that too."

"That really sucks, I mean do you have to take a date to the party?" she asked me as I took another drink of wine. "You could just go stag." That's my friend for you, it wouldn't faze her to go alone, but I would feel awkward standing alone at a party where everyone is coupled up.

"Austin Wilson asked me to if I wanted to go with him to the party?" I told her curling up with my knees under my chin. LeStat nudged my hand, so I started to absently pet him as he purred and curled up in my lap. "The man hardly speaks to me except to give me instructions or to check on my progress on a client. Suddenly he asks me out?"

"The cute biker you work with, that Austin??" Cara gasped. "What did you say?" I cringed because I knew she was going to give me shit when I told her.

"I said I couldn't believe he really wanted to take me to the party?" I mumbled under my breath." I thought back to the conversation and realized how bitchy I must have sounded. "He just looked at me funny and walked away."

I heard her car door slam and alarm beep, keys jingling as she opened her door. Her two dogs started barking loudly.

"I'm coming to get you in the morning for brunch and we are going to discuss this, but for now I need to take care of Spock and Kirk." I giggled when she talked about her dogs. She was a huge Star Trek fan and when she named her boxers after two main characters I about died laughing. "I will see you at ten and we will finish this talk over breakfast."

"Ok, pet the kiddies for me. Love you girl." I told her as she said it back and hung up. I got up and washed out my glass and plate deciding to make an early night of it. I had a lot to do this weekend and I wanted a clear head.

2

Gears

"Gears, get your ass in here." Undertaker hollered when he saw me outside. I was coming by to check on the books for the garage. Since Undertaker got married to Annie, she had been doing most of the bookkeeping, so I just checked it over. It saved me a lot of time and that was good because work had been super busy lately. I still handled the taxes and payroll, but she took care of the rest.

"I'm coming, where's the fire man?" I laughed. I saw Annie when I walked in behind the counter. "Where's Mattie?" I asked before I saw the pack and play behind the counter. Annie hopped down and came over to give me a hug.

"Keep it down, he is napping. I have some orders to get entered while I have time." She said as she started back to work. I peeked over and saw the baby sound asleep. I don't know what she was worried about, he could sleep through all the racket in the garage, I don't think I was going to wake him. The baby was adorable, he had his father's dark hair and his mother's bright blue eyes. He would be a heartbreaker for sure.

"I just came by to do payroll; I'll be back in the office." I told her as I walked past. She mumbled something and I kept going. Undertaker was in the office when I entered. "Hey man, everything ok?"

"Yeah, just tired. Mattie's sleep schedule is all messed up right now. I think we have had a good year. Axle and I talked; we would like to give the guys a bonus." He said as he rubbed the back of his neck. "Just a little something to show our appreciation."

"Okay, I'll check and let you know what a good number would be. It will save you on taxes as well." I told him as I sat down and fired up the computer. "I should only be a couple of hours tops. I'll find you when I'm finished."

"Sounds good, I have a bike I want to get some work done on before we head home for the day. I don't like to work weekends now, if I can help it." Undertaker said before pulling the office door closed behind him.

I settled in to work on the payroll. Although I had a full-time job, I helped keep the books for business' associated with the club. I liked to make sure everything was in order, and no one was trying to undercut us. Everyone contributed in different ways. Since I was good with numbers this was mine. My old man had been a member for years before he passed. I was patched in while he was still around. I grew up around the club and had my first bike when I was sixteen. I also had an old mustang that I drove for dates and when the weather was bad. Most people were surprised when they learned I was part of the Rippers MC. I knew I didn't really look the part. I wasn't covered in tats and while I was fit, I wasn't all muscled up. I could hold my own in a fight and I earned my cut the same as everyone else.

I wasn't really into the parties they had at the clubhouse. Fucking any available whore just didn't interest me. I avoided the clubhouse during those parties. I wanted someone that I could enjoy a conversation with, not just be physically attracted to. Sophie Boyd popped in my head. I don't know what it was about her, but she had my attention from her first day on the job. She was about 5'4, curvy figure with light brown hair. She wore it short around her face and she had the prettiest hazel eyes. She took almost an instant dislike to me, and I still could not figure out why. I tried to talk to her, but she was a bit hostile. I really should just give up, but it was not in my nature. She was like a puzzle I was determined to solve. I would have to think about that later. I had work to do. Diving back into the books I focused on that for a while.

A tap on the door had me looking up at Annie smiling holding little Mattie in her arms. I looked at the clock and realized it was just after twelve. I had been finishing up, so I shut down the computer and got up. I walked over and kissed the baby on top of his head.

"Are ya'll heading home?" I asked her as Undertaker came up behind her and nodded at me. "I'm done, payroll is ready you just have to print the checks and sign them. There is a little something extra for everyone too."

"Great. Don't forget we are having a club dinner next Saturday. You should bring someone?" Annie said smiling at me. I knew she wanted to see us happy, but I couldn't even get Sophie to give me the time of day. I really needed to let that go.

"I'll be there, don't know if I'm bringing anyone or not." I told her as I turned out the light and followed them out. I really needed to get out more and meet people. "See you both later."

I watched them drive away and then got on my bike to go home. I lived on the property in my Pops' old house. It was paid for and so I didn't have to worry about anything but utilities and upkeep. I also liked the privacy. Visitors had to be cleared through the gate now. We didn't get unwanted guests. Pulling up to the house I looked around and thought about how lonely it could be here sometimes. Walking in

I looked at the small tree I had in the corner by the fireplace. It was kind of sad looking. I had put some white lights on it, and I had a Santa hat as a topper but no ornaments. I enjoyed watching tv with just the lights from the tree on. My mom always loved Christmas so even though she was gone I made sure to have a tree up every year. I was getting hungry, so I fixed myself a sandwich and grabbed a bag of chips from the pantry along with a coke. Sitting down in my chair I opened my e-reader and started reading something from my list. The guys teased me about reading so much but it was relaxing. I was reading when my phone rang. I looked at the caller id and it was my partner at work. UGH not today. I chose to ignore it and let it go to voicemail. Most people at work didn't know it but I'm a silent partner. I don't want to be part of the managerial staff. I prefer to just do my job and let someone else be supervisor. I didn't know what Lee wanted but I wasn't in the mood to deal with him right now. Most of the time he ran things just fine on his own, but he had a bug up his butt about everyone bringing someone to this party. Hell, I didn't have anyone to bring either and I'm sure that is why he was calling. I decided to turn the ringer of my phone off.

The next morning, I woke up early and worked out in the clubhouse gym. After showering, I decided I wanted to go for a ride so I could grab a late breakfast at the diner in town.

I drove around for a while and saw a couple of guys in the diner. I figured I could stop and visit since I wasn't doing anything else. Pulling up, I climbed off my bike just as a car pulled in beside me. I looked up to see Sophie and the vet from the shelter get out of the car. I was going to say something, but they hadn't noticed me and were kind of arguing. I quietly followed them inside. Hawk saw me and waved me over to sit with them. The girls sat in a booth a couple down from where the guys were.

"Hey ya'll having breakfast." I asked as I sat down next to Rider. Hawk looked irritated and so did Fang. "What's going on?"

"Fang's sister is coming home from college for Christmas, and he is trying to warn us off." Hawk said laughing about it. Rider looked murderous. "Like we would disrespect him like that."

"Katherine is too good for the likes of any of us. I want her to finish school and find a nice doctor or accountant to marry." Fang grumbled. I choked out a laugh as he seemed to forget that was exactly what I am. Hawk smirked as he caught on to why I was laughing.

"Well hell Fang, let me know when you want me to take her out." I said with a smirk. He looked like he was about to come across the table when I raised my eyebrow at him. "You did say an accountant. That's what I do for a living, remember?"

"Asshole, you know what I meant." He said eating his hashbrowns. "I just want her to do something with her life."

"Maybe you should let Katie decide what she wants. I seem to remember her being pretty independent and stubborn." Rider said as he got up and went to pay for his lunch. I watched him leave and frowned. Rider was a loner and he kept his sex life private. Katie was twenty-six finishing up medical school and starting her residency in the fall. She was old enough to decide who she wanted to date and I'm sure she would not appreciate her brother's interference.

"What the hell was that about?" Hawk said as we watched him leave. "What are you doing here, you usually hang at your place on Saturday afternoons unless we have a ride?'

"I was restless so I figured I would go for a ride while the sun was out, and we weren't buried in snow." I said as I ordered a coffee and an omelet. I sat back and watched Sophie talking to her friend. She looked so frustrated I wanted to help. I could hear their conversation now that the guys were quiet.

"Why didn't you say yes when he asked you out?" her friend asked her. She blushed and shook her head.

"Why would he want to go out with me? I'm overweight, quiet and I snap at the poor man every time he talks to me. I don't get it." She said flushed. I could not believe that is how she saw herself. I thought she was beautiful, and I liked her curves. I didn't want to date a stick figure; I like my women to be soft. I want something to hold on to and cuddle with. She was perfect just the way she was. I was about to get up and tell her so when she looked up and spotted me. Her eyes got wide as saucers and her face was the color of a fire truck. I tried to pretend I had not heard their conversation, but she caught me looking dead at her.

"What is it, Sophie? Your face turned red as a beet." Her friend followed her gaze and turned around to see me staring. "Oh, is that him?"

"Yes, that's him. I'm not hungry anymore. Can you just take me home please?" Sophie said with a defeated look on her face. I didn't like that at all. I excused myself and got up to walk over to the table. She stood up and walked right into my chest. I caught her before she stumbled. She looked up at me and we were so close I could have kissed her, and I wanted to, so badly.

"I'm sorry Sophie, I didn't mean to eavesdrop on your conversation. I was having breakfast talking to my friends and they were so busy eating they stopped talking." I apologized to her, and she blinked a minute and then stepped back. "I would like to give you a ride home so we can talk."

"I don't think that is such a good idea Mr. Wilson. I'm sorry we were talking about you." She looked mortified. "I'll see you at work on Monday." I gently grabbed her elbow to stop her from walking away.

"Please?" I asked as she looked at me again. Her friend said something in her ear and left. Her mouth dropped as she watched her friend leave.

"Well, um I guess I need a ride now anyway. Thanks." She stammered glancing at the door again. I reached for her jacket and helped her put it on.

"Let's go." I said as we walked outside. She stopped when she saw my motorcycle. "You can wear my helmet. I promise it will be safe."

"Ok, I've never ridden before." She said biting her lip. She looked so cute I couldn't wait to have her on my bike. I fastened my helmet on her and then climbed on the bike. I held my hand out to her.

"Just throw your leg over and wrap your arms around my waist. Keep your feet on the bars. If I lean, you lean with me." I told her as she climbed on behind me. She wrapped her arms around my waist, and I pressed her hands to me with one of my own. "Hold on tight. Where do you live?" "Liberty Ridge, I have an apartment in one of the restored homes." She told me as she tightened her grip. I nodded and took off towards her place. I felt how tense she was but after a few minutes she seemed to relax against me. I had never had a woman on the back of my bike before. It meant something to let one ride with you. This woman made me nuts, she was always so confrontational at work and a little hostile. I wasn't sure why unless it was competitiveness. I pulled up to the row of remodeled homes that had been turned into duplexes and quads, stopping to ask which one was hers.

"I'm in the third one. It's small but it's functional." She said as I pulled up to her place and parked. She held on to me as she swung her leg over and stepped off. I climbed off and pulled the helmet off of her securing it to my bike.

"I can remember when these were single family homes. I guess they got too expensive to keep up that way." I said as I followed her to her door. She was on the second floor, which I found comforting. We went inside and she laid her purse on her kitchen counter. She turned to look at me with a frown. I wanted to know why she hated me so much.

3

Sophie

I stared at Austin Wilson standing in my apartment. I didn't know what to think. I never thought he would be at my place. I was suddenly really happy that I was a bit of a neat freak. I would have been mortified if there had been laundry, panties or bra's laying around. Thankfully everything was in its place.

"I appreciate the ride home, but I'm not really sure what we could have to talk about." I said as I sat on one of the stools. I glanced down and rubbed my jeans. Austin sighed and pulled out a stool and sat down beside me. About that time my cat decided he wanted attention and started to rub against his legs. He glanced down and gave the cat some scratches.

"I want to know what I have done to make you hate me so much." Austin said as he looked into my eyes. He had such pretty eyes, like melted chocolate. I blinked and tried to look away. "You won't talk to me at work except to snap at me or tell me to go away."

"I'm working hard to keep up with all my accounts and it seems like you always have time to hang around my desk. I guess I wondered if you were trying to steal away any of my accounts." I whispered. I felt bad after I said it. I mean really, maybe he just worked faster than I did.

"I really just wanted to offer you help if it was needed. I have been working there for years and you are right out of school. Your first job in your chosen field. I'm sorry if you thought I was competing." He said as he reached over for my hand. "I have a few jobs I do for the MC as well, so I work late a lot."

"I'm sorry, I jumped to conclusions. It was just my own insecurities making me act like a raging bitch. I don't know why you bother trying to be friendly to me. I sure haven't made it easy on you." I mumbled frowning again. I don't know why this man was in my apartment. He was so cute and sexy in a nerdy kind of way. Not to mention, him on that bike made his sexy factor shoot through the roof. Holding on to him during that ride had me wet and a bit uncomfortable.

"Well, first I think you are beautiful, and I have wanted to ask you out for months. Second, I figured you might be insecure about your job, so I tried not to take it personally. I guess when you shot me down after work, I didn't know what to say to you, so I just walked away." He said as he looked at me. "When I heard what you said to your friend all I could think about was getting up and kissing you."

"Yeah right, because guys like you really want chubby girls like me." I scoffed at him and got up. I was going to try to show him to the door but when he got up, he circled an arm around my waist and pulled me to him. Slipping his other hand in my hair he leaned in and kissed me. It wasn't a peck or a small kiss either. He pressed his lips to mine and then ran his tongue along my lower lip until I opened up for him. He slid his tongue inside my mouth and tangled with mine. I felt it down to my clit. I wrapped my arms around his neck and kissed him back sucking on his pouty lower lip. He started to kiss down my neck and to my shoulder then stepped back and looked me in the eyes. I knew I was flushed and breathing hard. I must look a mess.

"God, you are the most beautiful, luscious woman I have ever seen. I don't know how you see yourself but believe me when I say that I want you." He said as he leaned forward and kissed me again gently. "I need to go; I have some things to take care of, but I would really like to see you again outside of work. Will you let me take you to dinner tomorrow night?"

I was touching my lips, eyes wide still staring at him in shock. I have never been kissed like that in my life. Hell, I've only had sex once and it was nothing to write home about. I must have been staring because he frowned and grabbed his coat.

"I'm sorry, clearly I've overstepped." He said as I realized he was going to leave. I stumbled over to him and grabbed his arm to stop him from leaving. "Are you okay, Sophie?"

"Yes, I'd like to have dinner with you tomorrow and yes, I'm okay. You just took me by surprise. I'm not mad and you didn't overstep." I said blushing and looking down at where I had a hold on his jacket. I quickly released him and stepped back. I looked up and he was smiling at me. He had a great smile, I didn't see it that often, but I guess that was my fault for always being so mean. "What time and what should I wear?"

"I thought we would do something casual so that we are comfortable. Anything you wear is going to be lovely. I'll pick you up at six." He said as he kissed my cheek and left. I stood there at the main door and watched him mount his bike and ride off. I sat down and picked up my cat stroking his head more for my own comfort than his.

What the hell just happened? I went from not being able to stand the man to kissing him and agreeing to a date. Huh, this calls for some wine. I'll call and see if Cara wants to come over, order pizza and share a bottle. I went back in and grabbed my phone to text her because I was too flustered to talk about it yet. It was still too early so we agreed she would be here about five-thirty with the pizza, and I had soft drinks as well as a bottle of Moscato we could have. Looking at the clock I figured I had time to do some laundry before she came over. Walking into my bedroom, I grabbed the dirty clothes and started a load then went back to try and decide what I could wear tomorrow. It was really cold and was supposed to start snowing soon. I decided on a pair of stretchy cream-colored leggings and a burgundy sweater. I had a pair of black thigh high boots that would complete the outfit. I pulled out some lacy under garments to wear with it. I didn't plan on anything happening tomorrow but just in case I wanted to feel sexy. Since I wasn't leaving the house again today, I decided to hop in the shower, shave everything and put on some pajamas. May as well be comfortable when Cara got here. I texted and told her to bring her jammies and she could just crash here tonight. We had not had a movie night in a while. I pulled out some paper plates and a couple of wine glasses when I heard the doorbell.

I walked over, checked the peephole and then let her in. I took the pizza in her hand and put it on the counter as she dropped her overnight bag by the couch.

"Well hell, let me go get in my pajamas and we can get cozy, eat and watch movies." Cara said as she headed to my room to change. I received a text from Austin a few minutes later.

Austin: Looking forward to tomorrow night. I hope you won't change your mind.

Me: I am too, and I won't. How did you get my number?

Austin: I asked Lee for it. Told him I had a work question for you.

Me: Clever, I have my friend Cara over, so I will see you tomorrow.

Austin: Goodnight.

"Hey, what's that smile for? Who are you talking to?" Cara asked as she plopped down on the couch and grabbed a plate with some pizza on it. LeStat loved Cara so he immediately jumped on he couch and curled up beside her to go to sleep.

"Oh, that's part of why I suggested you come over. You will not believe what happened earlier." I told her blushing again. I couldn't stop thinking about that kiss.

"You mean after the cute biker drove you home?" she winked at me. I took a long drink of my wine and put the glass down. "I thought you hated him."

"I did too, but I guess it wasn't 'hate' that I was feeling. I thought he was an arrogant ass who was lazy and was trying to take credit for other people's work." I took another drink of my wine and refilled my glass. "I was stupid and mean. Insecurity reared its ugly head and turned me into a hateful bitch monster. I'm so embarrassed Cara. He was just trying to help me."

"What about him asking you to the party?" she asked me, giggling. "He seemed plenty interested when he jumped up and stalked over to our table." I know my cheeks were flaming red. Her eyes got big, and she put down her glass. "Ok, you have something to tell me because your face is the color of a fire engine."

I bit my lip as I remembered that amazing kiss, he laid on me earlier today. The way he manhandled me pulling me into his arms and kissing me like he wanted to devour me. I took a deep breath and looked at my hands.

"Cara, first the ride was amazing. I have never been on a motorcycle in my life and riding wrapped around him with my arms around his waist was an amazing experience. Then he walks me inside and insists on clearing the air about our work relationship. Then suddenly he tells me I'm beautiful and kisses the daylight out of me. Now we are going out on a date tomorrow." I look up at her and she is speechless. I drain my glass of wine and pour another one.

"You have a date with your arch nemesis from work, the guy you have been hating on since you started working there?" she repeated as she stared at me for confirmation. I nodded, trying to eat some pizza to soak up the alcohol coursing through my system. "Wow!"

"Did I mention I always thought he was sexy? I mean he isn't the typical biker with bulked out muscles and tattoos everywhere, but he has a smart mysteriousness about him, and those eyes are just so pretty. Girl, he was smiling and laughing earlier today. I had to shower and change when he left." I told her giggling. "He's part of that MC in town, those guys look all rough and dangerous. I don't know what he could be mixed up in. I probably shouldn't date him. I think I'll call and cancel."

"NO, you will do no such thing. You haven't been on a date in so long you probably have cobwebs on your damn lady parts. Also, I only ever hear good stuff about most of them. They keep the crime down around here. I don't know what all they are in to but I'm sure you are perfectly safe with him." Cara said firmly. "Besides you need a date for the Christmas party and your parents Christmas dinner, you could take him."

"You want me to take a biker to my parents' house?" I asked her shocked. "I mean can you see their faces when we ride up on his Harley?" I pictured it and suddenly couldn't stop laughing. We both broke down in a fit of giggles.

"I'm sure he owns a regular vehicle too, and he works with you, so you know he cleans up nice." She countered. I put my drink down and looked at her while thinking about it. That would certainly shut them up. Maybe I could get some peace if I brought a date. "He is obviously into you Soph."

"Let's see how tomorrow goes first. I have to get through a date with him before I decide on asking him to deal with my crazy family." I said as I put another slice of pizza on my plate. "Enough serious talk, let's watch Magic Mike." I pulled a blanket over me on the couch and curled my feet under me, turning on the movie. That's how we spent the rest of the evening, movies, snacks before falling asleep on the couch.

4

Gears

Leaving Sophie was the hardest thing I had done in a long time, but it was too soon to be throwing her over my shoulder and giving her a good seeing to. I know that I am not your average biker. I have a couple of tattoos, but they are where I can hide them for work. I don't work out to the extent that most of the guys do, but I am in good shape. I am the brains of the club, not to say the other guys aren't smart, they just don't have my level of knowledge with numbers. Since I co-own the accounting firm I work at, I get by with just a few accounts to make it believable that I should be there. Most of my accounts are club related. I was heading to the compound for a meeting with Axle and Blade about our holiday festivities. We always did a big toy drive for the children's wing of the hospital in town. Liberty University Hospital wasn't the largest, but they had some great physicians and we liked to make sure they had what they needed so we held fundraisers throughout the year and had a toy drive for the children's wing for the kids that had to stay in the hospital.

22

I pulled up in front of the clubhouse and parked my bike. Looking up at the sky I could tell we were going to be getting snow soon so I wanted to ride while I could. I secured my bike, took off my helmet and walked inside the clubhouse. There were a couple of guys at the kitchen counter having some dinner. Lillian, one of the widowed old ladies was taking care of cooking for us. She felt safe here after her old man died during a raid. She has a small house out back. She is still young and attractive, so the guys watch out for her. Fury looked up at me and jerked his head toward the office where Axle and Blade were waiting for me. I stopped and gave Lillian a hug.

"Hey beautiful, will you fix me one of those when we get done with our meeting?" I asked her as I pointed at the steak and fries on Fury's plate. I was starving. She kissed me on the cheek and shooed me away.

"Of course, I will, now scoot the guys are waiting and they want dinner too." Lillian said as she turned to get more food from the fridge. I winked at her, and Fury growled. I glanced at him in surprise. He looked at Lillian again and his eyes softened. Well, I'll be damned, he is sweet on her. I walked across the common room down the hall to the Prez's office. I walked in and the guys jerked their heads at me. I sat down on the leather couch by the door.

"What's up guys?" I asked casually since I didn't know if this was about anything specific or just an update on the Christmas drive. Blade handed me some papers. I looked at them and frowned. It looked like the manager of Trixie's was skimming money off the top. I read the reports and the more I read the madder I got. There was a reason I did the books for our business. This is one of them.

"What the fuck is Richie thinking?" I cursed, looking closer to the report they handed me. "Did he think I wouldn't see this?"

"Bethann came by earlier today and showed us. She said she thought the deposits had been light for the weekend shift the last couple of weeks, so she started talking to the girls. Turns out the numbers they gave her did not match up with what was being deposited. They also said that Richie had been taking a bigger cut of their tip money this past month. Candy has a toddler and a useless ex-boyfriend who doesn't pay child support. She needs every bit of money she makes." Blade growled under his breath. He helped bounce at the club when they were shorthanded, and he had free time from his construction job. Both Axle and Blade used to work with Masters' Construction, but Axle stopped taking jobs when he stepped up in the club. Blade still did some when the weather was nice. He liked the manual labor and the extra money. Rubbing my hand over my face I groaned.

"Okay, I'm going to head over to the club after dinner tonight. I'd like Fury and Hawk to come with me. I have a date tomorrow and I don't need to have bruises all over my fists the first time I take my lady out." Axle chucked at me when I said it. Blade grinned. I'm going to be hearing about this.

"No problem, Blade text Hawk and have him meet Gears at the club around ten thirty, we will tell Fury now. Everything is looking good for the holiday gift drive. I'm going to send a couple of prospects by the businesses to pick up the collections and then I'll have a few of the club whores do the wrapping. We have a list of things the kids asked Santa for, I made sure to pick those up. The rest will be wrapped according to age and sex of the child and distinguished by the type of wrapping paper. We will deliver them Christmas morning. Undertaker is going to play Santa as always." Axle said as he got up and we walked out of his office. "Let's eat, I'm starved."

We went in and grabbed a couple of beers and sat down at the long table by the kitchen. Fury came over and sat down with us while we filled him in on the situation. Lillian came over and put our plates down avoiding Fury while she did it. I can't believe that I had missed the tension between them. Lillian's old man was gunned down a couple of years ago. She was a beautiful woman. She was about five feet five inches, a nice figure although a bit on the thin side lately with her black hair in a pixie cut around her face. Her eyes were a pale blue, and she was gorgeous. We all gave her a wide berth as she was a widow, and we respected our women. Fury's eyes tracked her every move. I'd think about that later.

"So, Fury I'm heading to Trixie's around ten-thirty. I'm going to want you and Hawk there to help me send a message to Richie. He's been skimming and stealing money from the dancers." I told him as I cut into my steak. He looked surprised for a minute and nodded.

"What do you need us for? I've seen you fight you can handle him." Fury said frowning. He never minded roughing up someone who deserved it. I rolled my eyes as I saw Axle and Blade smirking. Well damn here goes.

"Pretty boy here finally got that girl at his firm to go out with him and he doesn't want to mess up his hands." Blade teased as he worked on his food. I flipped him off and frowned.

"Hell Fury, you love to rough up traitors and it's Christmas time. I'm a giver. Just say thanks." I threw back at him. He laughed out loud, and I almost dropped my fork. It was just not a sound we heard much anymore. I couldn't help it, I smiled at him shaking my head.

"Hawk messaged me, he will be there. He was going to be covering at the door anyway." Axle said as he finished off his beer. "Fill me in on how it goes. I'm heading to my room. Jasmine will be here in about half an hour have someone send her straight to my room." He got up and walked away. Axle enjoyed the club life. He had not had a girlfriend since we were younger when he was with Bear's sister Valkyrie. What happened to her changed him, and he didn't date. He took what he was offered when he needed it and that was it. The club girls knew not to knock on his door or touch him unless it was invited. The one time one of them did they got banned. I had a couple of hours to kill before we headed to the club, so I headed back to my place on the back of the property. I had a cabin style house, two bedrooms and two bathrooms open concept, so the kitchen flowed with the living room. The fireplace was used a lot as it got cold as hell here in Colorado. I didn't want to start one since I would be leaving in a couple of hours. I planned to bring Sophie here tomorrow and cook for her. Looking around the place was clean, so I just started some laundry and looked to see what I needed from the store. I figured I would fix some lasagna, a salad and some garlic bread. I would have leftovers for a few days after. I went and changed into some leathers and long sleeve flannel and my cut. I looked at the tree in the corner, I had put lights on it but had not bothered with ornaments. Normally I did that with my sister Dawn, but she wasn't going to be able to come home from school. I could see if Sophie wanted to help me decorate. We could have dinner, play some Christmas music and decorate the tree. I think that would be a nice first date.

I put up my clothes and slipped the grocery list in my wallet then headed out for the club. It was about twenty minutes from the compound. It was cold as hell, so I took my mustang. I hated not riding but I wasn't trying to get sick. It was one thing when the sun was beating down, but the weather was changing fast, we were about to have a rough winter. I warmed up my baby. She was a beauty, a candy apple red 1967 classic Mustang. I had helped restore her myself with the help of Taker and the guys. Driving over to the club I smiled thinking about my date with Sophie tomorrow. It took me months to get her to speak to me, then it was all verbal sparring with her. Normally I would have been turned off but something about her just stayed with me. I'm glad I finally broke through and found out why she had been so hostile. I still can't believe she thought she was unattractive or fat. Fuck that, she was beautiful, soft and sexy as hell. I didn't go for barbie types. I wanted a real woman, not someone who watched every bite they put in their mouth. No thank you.

I parked outside the club and Fury pulled up beside me. He was on his bike, but he was also a masochist. Hawk was already here. We walked in and he looked pointedly at the office. Calling one of the other bouncers over to cover the door, he followed behind us. Hawk was about six feet with a shaved head and a stubble goatee. He was a physical trainer during the day and was cut with a very defined six pack. You just knew you shouldn't fuck with him. The man could be a teddy bear but if you pissed him off, he could snap you in half. He and Fury together were a fearsome sight. We pushed the door to the office open without knocking to find Richie sniffing a line of coke. Fury growled and slammed his head on the desk.

"What the fuck Richie, you know we don't allow that shit in here?" Hawk grabbed some rope from the cabinet behind the desk and tied him to the chair. Fury cracked his knuckled and rolled his neck. I saw the twinkle in his eye. Oh boy, it was going to get ugly.

"Lock the door Gears, shits about to get real." Fury said in a dead tone. Thankfully the office was soundproof, the floor was tile for easy clean up. "So, you little shit, you are not only doing drugs on the Rippers' property but you're stealing too. How fucking stupid are you to be stealing from an MC?" Hawk grabbed his hand and started breaking his fingers one at a time. The man screamed like a baby.

"I'm sorry, I'll never do it again. Please stop." Richie begged like the little bitch he was. Hawk punched him in the face. Blood spurted from his broken nose and Fury grabbed his favorite knife from his boot.

"You're right, you will never do it again. You were told when we hired you. No drugs and no disrespecting the girls. They work hard for their money. We get a twenty percent cut of their tips and they keep eighty. When you started taking thirty and pocking ten you fucked up, but then you had to start shorting the deposits as well." Fury took his knife and cut the shirt off then started cutting the word thief into the man's chest. Glancing up he saw the look on Hawk's face. Hawk was protective of all the dancers, but he had a special fondness for Bethann. Candy was her sister and so her kids were Bethann's family. You don't fuck with family. His face was cold as ice as he wrapped his meaty palm around Ritchie's arm with one hand and held his hand out for the knife with the other. Fury gave an evil smile and handed the knife to his brother. Hawk carved pussy into the man's bicep. I walked over to the cabinet and grabbed some rubbing alcohol. Not to disinfect it but because it would hurt. I opened it and poured some on his cuts as he paled and was breaking out into a sweat. I really hated people like him. Greedy and lazy. I wanted in on this little torture session.

"Stand his ass up for a minute, guys I want some of this." Fury and Hawk held him up and stood to either side while I kicked his right knee, breaking it. Then I took the knife and stabbed it right through his left foot. I looked at the piece of shit whimpering and noticed he had a diamond earring in his ear. I figured he bought it with the stolen money, so I ripped it out. The man passed out from the pain and the guys dropped his ass right there on the floor. "What a fucking mess. Take him out the back door and get rid of him. Keep the office door locked and have Gator come clean it up. I don't want Bethann to see any of this. I'm heading home."

5

Sophie

I woke up to the smell of bacon and pancakes cooking. I rubbed my eyes and looked at the clock. It was already ten thirty in the morning. I threw off my covers and walked into the kitchen to see the couch already cleaned up and Cara making us breakfast. LeStat swirling and purring around her feet.

"You didn't have to do that, we could have gone and got something." I told her as my stomach growled. She winked as she fixed us both a plate and set them on the table. I poured myself some coffee and refilled hers before sitting down. "Thanks, this looks delicious."

Cara laughed at me. We had been best friends for years. I knew she was going to head to the shelter when we finished eating. She was a workaholic and loved animals. Maybe if things worked out with Austin, I could fix her up with someone too.

"You know I have to go by the clinic and check on the animals. I have a couple of pregnant dogs. I want to check on them and be sure they are okay. I also have to feed them since we are short staffed through the holidays. It won't be so bad after Christmas. I have a couple of college kids coming to work with me. They want to intern with me since I work with large animals as well as small." Cara was animated when she talked about animals. She truly loved her job. I wish that I loved my job as much as she does hers, but at least mine doesn't take up all my free time.

"Ok, well try to at least get some rest and don't over do it. If you need help call me." I told her as she started to get up to take the plates to the kitchen. "No ma'am, you cooked I clean. Now get."

"Fine, but no way am I calling you, date remember???" she smirked at me as she picked up her overnight bag. I walked her to the door and watched her drive off in her truck. That thing was as old as she was and it needed to be replaced. Oh well. I shook my head and closed the door. Heading to the kitchen to clean up from breakfast. When I finished, I started to head to my room to shower when my phone rang. I ran across the room to get it before they hung up.

"Hello?" I answered a little breathless. I heard a chuckle on the other end and knew it was Austin.

"Hey beautiful, just wanted to remind you that I would be picking you up at six and to be sure and dress comfortable." He said making me smile. I still couldn't believe he thought of me that way.

"I'll be ready. Just don't forget to call me and warn me if you change your mind." I told him biting my lip. I swear I heard him growl.

"Be ready, I will see you in a few hours." He said and then disconnected the call. Wow, he really didn't like me to be down on myself. I smiled and put on my Christmas music and then went to shower. I took my time making sure every bit of me was fresh as a daisy. Washed and dried my hair. It was only to my chin, so it didn't take long to dry it and fixing it was just a good brushing and a quick run with a hot iron. I only wore mascara and tinted lip balm. I walked out of my bathroom in my robe and looked in my closet. I decided on a pair of cream-colored leggings with a long brown sweater and some knee-high brown boots. Cute but comfortable. I headed to the living room and looked at the clock. It was only about three thirty. Good grief, what was I going to do for the next couple of hours. I picked up a few Christmas gifts last weekend. I could always wrap those and put them under the tree. I walked to my hall closet and pulled out some wrapping paper and got the tape from the kitchen along with some scissors. After getting the gifts out I started wrapping them up. I love to make them really pretty, so I used ribbons and bows. I make my own tags, so they are all personalized. Before I knew it, I heard a knock on my door. I glanced up and it was five minutes to six. Smiling, I stood up and went to check the peephole. I saw Austin standing there with flowers in his hand. I unlocked and opened the door to let him in. He leaned over and kissed my cheek handing me the bouquet of pink roses. I blushed as I took them.

"You look beautiful Sophie; I love those boots." He said as he took in my outfit and smiled.

"Thank you, these are beautiful. Come in while I put these in some water." I told him as I reached under the sink for a vase. Pouring some water in the vase, I took off the plastic and trimmed the ends, arranging them in the vase and putting them on my tv stand so I could see them. I couldn't resist leaning over to smell them. I sighed; I don't remember the last time a man bought me flowers.

"You okay baby?" he asked me as he came up behind me and wrapped his arms around my waist. I didn't even think at first, I just leaned back into him and wrapped my arms around his squeezed and then stepped away.

"I'm okay, just thinking about how long it's been since anyone bought me flowers, then realized nobody ever has." I looked up at him and bit my lip. He growled again. My eyes got wide as he leaned in and kissed me.

"Every time you bite your lip, I want to do it for you. I hope you don't mind me kissing you. I don't think I can stop." He said winking at me. "Are you ready?"

"Yes, I just need to grab my coat and purse." I told him as I took them off the hook by the door. He helped me into my coat like the gentleman he was and then with his hand on the small of my back led me out the door to his car. I had seen it in the parking lot at work, but I didn't realize it was his. I whistled.

"You like it, huh." He grinned like a teenage boy proud of his toy. I laughed at him. "What's your cat's name?"

"LeStat, I like vampire movies and I love it, it was always my dream car." I told him as he opened the door for me. He waited for me to swing my legs in before he closed the door. I watched him walk around and noticed he was wearing some very well-fitted jeans and a nice sweater under his leather coat. With the leather coat and jeans, I could see the biker along with the accountant. I glanced at my hands when he climbed in beside me and started the car. The engine purred and I was again entranced looking around the inside of the car. He drove towards the outskirts of town, and I looked at him with a question on my face.

"I hope you don't mind; I'm cooking dinner for you at my place, and I thought if you wanted to, we could decorate my tree. It has lights on it but no ornaments yet." He glanced at me to gauge my reaction.

"That sounds perfect. I love Christmas." I told him. He reached over and took my hand in his putting them on his thigh. I had butterflies in my stomach whenever he touched me. I was going to be a hot mess by the end of the night.

We pulled up to the gates of the compound and Austin reached out and punched in a code on the keypad. I had never been here before or even near the place. The gates opened and a younger handsome guy popped his head out of the guard shack to speak to Austin.

"Hey Gears, this your girl?" the guy in the leather cut said with a mischievous grin. He winked at me, and Austin frowned at him. I was embarrassed thinking he may not want them to think he is with me. Maybe that's why he brought me here instead of taking me out somewhere.

"Yes, and don't you forget it either. Hands and eyes off, understand Gator." He said firmly to the younger guy. Gator had the grace to blush and just nod at me stepping back into the shack. Austin looked over at me and narrowed his eyes. He had to let go of my hand to throw the car in park when he entered his code. He reached over and placed it back on his leg before driving toward the back of the property. He stopped in front of this cute cabin style house. It had a small porch with a couple of rocking chairs and a small table in between them. They looked wide and comfortable. Parking at the side he came around and opened the door to help me out. Putting his arm around my shoulders he led me to the door then opened it to lead me inside. I walked in and looked around. He had a fire going in the fireplace. I could smell what I would guess was lasagna cooking in the oven.

"I know what you're thinking. I am not the irresponsible as to leave the fire going and the oven on while I'm gone. I had one of the guys over here watching everything. He left when I pulled up to the gate. I didn't want you to be cold or have to wait for dinner to cook." Austin took my coat and put it on the coat hanger along with my purse.

6

Austin

I watched her look around my house and realized that for the first time I cared what someone thought of my home. It wasn't much but it had been our home when we were younger. It used to be a three bedroom but the one that had been next to the master was too small. It had been my room since Dawn needed the bigger closet. After Pop passed and my sister went off to school, I tore down the wall and expanded the master as well as remodeling the master bathroom. There was a small bathroom with a shower but mine had a large jacuzzi tub in it along with a walk-through shower. I also have a large closet now. I only use about a third of it, but I figured maybe one day I would have someone to share it with.

Sophie walked around the main room and looked at pictures I had on the mantel. I walked up behind her, and she was looking at the picture of me with my sister. It was taken last time she was here on break.

"That's my sister Dawn, she is off getting her law degree. She will be taking the bar soon so she decided not to come home for the holidays so she could study." I told her as I saw her smile at me.

"She looks nothing like you except for the eyes." She said as she looked at another one. That was the last family picture made before my mom passed. I was almost the spitting image of my Pop, Dawn took after our mother except for her eyes. She had bright-red hair, with freckles lining her little nose. She was very petite and built lean. Boys had always teased her in school because she had been built like a boy and was following me everywhere. "She looks like your mom except for the eyes. Where do your parents live?"

"They both passed. Ma passed about eight years ago, and Pop passed a couple years ago. He was never really the same after she died. I think sometimes he was waiting for me to finish school so I could be here to take care of Dawn." I said with a frown on my face. She looked horrified and I realized how that sounded. "Oh no baby, he didn't kill himself. He wrapped his bike around a tree driving on ice. I think he just stopped being as careful. He didn't see anyone else after she passed. This was our home."

"Oh goodness, I'm so sorry." She looked a little uncomfortable and I realized we had gotten into a deep conversation, and it was just our first date. Ugh what was wrong with me. I had verbal vomit around her.

"I'm going to put the bread in, it will only take a couple of minutes. What would you like to drink? I have coke, beer, wine or juice." I said as I walked toward the kitchen. I turned, not realizing she had followed me into the kitchen and was right behind me. She bumped into my chest and looked up at me. I kissed her forehead and put the bread into the oven, pulling the lasagna out.

"Juice please. I had too much wine last night so I should refrain since we have work tomorrow." She said smiling. I took a couple of glasses out and poured her some juice and myself a coke. I wasn't going to drink if she wasn't. "You can have a beer if you want, I don't care."

"I'm good sweetness, have seat and I'll have the food on the table in a second." I told her as I fixed our plates and put the bread on a plate in the middle of the table. I sat down and she took a deep breath licking her lips. I groaned and she glanced up at me. I just smiled and shook my head. I held the bread plate out for her and was surprised to see her grab two slices. Most women ate like birds. I liked that she had a healthy appetite. I put a couple on my plate as well and waited for her to try her lasagna. She cut off a piece and took a bite. I could see the pleasure on her face as she chewed. She took a bite of the bread after and looked at me surprised.

"Oh my God, Austin, this is so good. Did you make this from scratch?" she asked me with wide eyes. She was so cute and sexy and gorgeous. Lord I was in so much trouble with her.

"Yes, my mother made sure we could both cook. I enjoy it, although I don't do it often when it's just me. I made enough to have leftovers for a few days." I said as I started on my own dinner. We ate like that in companionable silence. It was nice being able to enjoy someone's company and not feel the need to fill the quiet with mindless chatter. When we finished eating, she started to get up and take her plate to the kitchen. I stopped her and shook my head. Taking the plate from her hand.

"Baby, go sit on the couch and I'll bet there in a minute." I told her as I rinsed our dishes and placed them in the microwave. I separated the leftovers into four containers. I was going to send two of them home with her. After the kitchen was cleaned up, I put on some Christmas music. She looked over at me and smiled. I would do anything to keep that smile on her face. When she smiled it lit up her face and shined from her eyes. I'm going to make her see herself the way I see her.

"I would have been glad to help you clean up. You cooked." She said as I stood in front of her and put the box of ornaments on the ottoman.

"Baby, you are a guest. Guests don't clean my house. Now I will let you help me decorate this tree." I winked at her and held my hands out to help her up. We started to put the ornaments on the tree. Some had special meaning. She pulled out one that was a mini leather cut.

"My dad had that made for me the year I was patched in. It was his way of telling me." I told her as I put the ornament on the tree. I pulled one of a stack of books. "This one was my sister's way of telling my dad she got accepted to law school."

"That is so neat, my mother has all of my childhood ornaments. The ones on my tree I bought for myself." I told him as I hung a couple of pretty glass ball ornaments. We went along like that until we finished. We stepped back to admire the tree. He suddenly pulled out his phone and turned us around taking a selfie of the two of us in front of his tree. Then he sent it to me.

"Awe, that is a cute picture. Thank you." I pulled on his shirt so he would lean down so I could kiss him. Laying his phone on the tv stand he wrapped his arms around me and pulled me closer. He kissed me again and then kissed my nose and stepped back.

"May I have this dance?" I said as I took her hand. The music was still playing. The song was *I'll be home for Christmas*. I pulled her into my arms and slowly danced her around the room. She laid her head on my chest, and I had mine on her head. She smelled like heaven. I can't remember having a better date in my life. When the song was over, she stepped back and she was flushed. So damn beautiful. I would be patient though. I really liked her.

"It's getting late, I should probably take you home." I said as I helped her into her coat. "I would really like it if you would attend the Christmas party with me."

"I think I would like that." Sophie smiled as I helped her into the car. The fire had died down enough I knew security would keep an eye on the house. I drove her home holding her hand the entire way. When we pulled in front of her place, I helped her out and walked her to her door. She unlocked the door, opened it and then turned to me.

"I had a great time tonight. That was the best date I have ever had, and dinner was delicious." she said as she bit that lip again looking down. I lifted her chin and kissed her goodnight.

"I will see you in the morning. Hope you sleep well; don't worry about lunch I have enough leftovers for the both of us." I told her. "Go ahead and lock your door while I'm standing here so I know your safe."

She smiled at me as she closed the door. I heard the lock engaged so I left. I saw her peek out of the curtain as I got into my car. I waved at her, and she waved back. That went even better than I expected. I drove back home and could not stop thinking about her lips or the way those leggings clung to her perfect full ass or those legs. I was hard as a rock. I knew I wasn't going to sleep until I took care of it. I stripped down and turned on the shower. I stepped in and grabbed the body wash. I liberally poured some into my hand and put in on my cock. Leaning on my arm on the tile and my head on my arm I started to stroke myself with the other. I pictured her beautiful face with that adorable haircut, the smell of her. She smelled like coconut and her skin was soft, her lips like full pillows that I love to bite and suck into my mouth. I could kiss her for hours. I kept stroking and pictured her in here with me on her knees with her mouth on my cock. Her tongue dancing around the head before she took me deep into her mouth. I started stroking faster and imagined myself coming down her throat as she swallowed everything that I gave her. Then I was spraying the wall with ropes of my cum. When I was spent, I washed off and got out of the shower. Climbing into my bed I looked at the picture of us in front of the tree and smiled. I made it my screen saver. Plugging up my phone I turned out the light. I was so relaxed that I was asleep in moments.

7

Sophie

I closed the door and locked it. Then walked over to the window to watch him leave. I know, I sound like a teenager. He was so sweet tonight. I never expected such a wonderful first date. He planned it out, brought me flowers, cooked me dinner and had a cute activity planned for us. He was affectionate but not groping or pushy. He clearly didn't expect me to put out on the first date. For a biker, he really was a gentleman. I'm so glad I agreed to go. I hung up my coat and purse. Then slipped off my boots. I went to take care of my nightly ritual of brushing my teeth and washing my face. I slipped off my clothes and crawled into my bed. LeStat curled up against my back. I pulled up the picture he took of us and looked at it again. It was so cute. I thought about making it my lock screen but didn't want him to think I was jumping into something too quickly. Turning out the light, I sent Cara a message that I would call her after work tomorrow. I just said it went great, but I was tired. She sent me a thumbs up emoji. Turning it over, I curled up to my extra pillow and fell asleep.

The next morning, I woke up in a great mood. I could not stop smiling. I took a quick shower and got ready for work then fixed myself some coffee and toast. I took some yogurt to eat on my break. I got my coat and purse then headed out the door. I pulled up and saw that Austin was sitting in his car. He looked up and smiled at me. Getting out of his car, he walked over and opened my door for me. I blushed and climbed out of the car. I saw that he had a thermal food container.

"This is our lunch; would you consider eating with me in my office today?" Austin asked as he opened the office door for me. "I figured that way we could talk openly."

We walked over to my desk, and I put my purse in my bottom drawer and locked it. I sat down and looked up at him. He looked so handsome in slacks and a button-down shirt. He had on a Christmas red tie that looked great with his skin tone.

"Sure, I'd like that. I usually eat around noon." I told him as I fired up my computer and checked my email. I glanced up at him and he was still smiling at me.

"I'll intercom you at noon, lunch will already be heated. What would you like to drink?" he asked me. "I have some bottled water or soda in my mini fridge in the office if that's okay."

"I usually drink water so that's perfect. Thanks." I said, blushing as Mr. Heath walked past my desk. Austin chuckled and walked to his office. I let out a deep breath. I sure hope I will be able to concentrate today. That man was going to be a distraction. I looked up to see Brittni, our receptionist giving me a nasty glare. I raised my eyebrow at her and then went back to work. She was always trying to get attention, so I guess she was mad that Austin was paying attention to me and not her. I didn't like her anyway, so I really didn't care. She had been a bitch to me since I started working here and I had done nothing to her.

I had a new client coming at ten-thirty to discuss me doing his business taxes. At about ten-fifteen my phone beeped, and it was Brittni telling me my new client was in the conference room. I locked my computer and picked up my notebook to go greet him. I walked into the conference room where Mr. Lewis was sitting with a cup of coffee. I walked over and shook his hand. I immediately wanted to snatch it back and go wash my hands. This man made me uncomfortable. I couldn't put my finger on why. He wasn't a bad looking man; he was well dressed but he just felt off.

"Mr. Lewis, I'm Sophie Boyd. Let's see what you are looking for, so I know if we are the right fit for you." I said and sat across the table from him and opened my notepad. He laid out a folder on the desk and we talked about his business and what he was looking for in an accountant. I was having lunch with Austin and wanted to be finished in time to go scrub my hands. UGH.

"I run RAVE Magazine. I have been looking to change some things up and go in a different direction. I am lining up some models and want to know how to maximize my deductions for the next quarter." He said as he stared at my chest. I narrowed my eyes on him.

"If you would like to leave your portfolio here, I can work on it and let you know what you would have to pay the first of the year." I said as I watched him. He stood up and walked around the table to me. The man had the nerve to put his hand on my shoulder.

"I just bet you can do plenty." He said in a smarmy voice. I almost gagged. I pushed my chair away from him and got up opening the door. "Would you like to have dinner with me to discuss it."

"I don't date clients and I'm seeing someone right now anyway." I said firmly. I saw Austin behind the man with a scowl on his face. "I will email you the figures after the first of the year. Please excuse me but I have another appointment."

I walked out of the conference room leaving him standing there looking shocked and a bit angry. What an asshole!! He probably thought I would be easy since I was on the chubby side. Jerk! I walked past Austin straight to the lady's room. I felt so unclean. I scrubbed my hands with hot water and soap until they were red. I gasped as Austin walked into the lady's room and locked the door.

"Baby, what did that man say to you. You looked furious and upset. I overheard him ask you out?" he said as he took some paper towels from the dispenser, turned the water on cold and held my hands under it for a minute before turning it off and drying my hands. Then he pulled me into his arms. "I sure hope I'm the one you're seeing."

I looked up at him and nodded. I wrapped my arms around his waist, and he leaned down and kissed me gently. "He just gives me the creeps; he kept staring at my chest and then had the nerve to touch my shoulder. I wanted to go take the hottest shower on the planet, but I can't leave work in the middle of the day." I felt his arms tighten around me.

"It's almost time for lunch, let's go to my office and eat. I'll try to take your mind off of this. We don't need his business, if you don't want to work with him don't. I promise it will be fine." he said as he rubbed my back, soothing me. I stepped back and looked up at him. How did I ever think this man was arrogant. He has been nothing but kind to me.

"Sounds good, I'll just go put his file on my desk." I said as I unlocked the bathroom door. He waited for me to leave first and then he followed me out. I went back to the conference room and thankfully the horrid man was gone. I picked up the file and placed it in my desk drawer. I will look at it tomorrow. I turned around to head to Austin's office when I bumped into Brittni.

"Do you even know who that was???" she asked me incredulously. "That man runs one of the most popular fashion magazines in the country. He was listed as one of the sexiest men in the state last year."

"So, you date him." I said as I walked around her to Austin's office. She really needed to back off and get a life. I was getting really tired of her crap. Austin was waiting for me and closed the door, locking it as I sat down at the table in the corner of his office. I looked around. I had never actually been in his office before. I think it was as big as Mr. Heath's office. He smiled and popped our food in the microwave then handed me a bottle of water from his fridge.

"Thank you." I said opening the bottle and taking a long drink. He pulled out the heated dishes and handed one to me. "I'm glad you brought this, it was so good last night, but lasagna is always better the next day."

"Agreed. I'm glad you liked it. I had a wonderful time with you. Thanks for helping me decorate my tree." he said, smiling as he started eating. We ate and chatted about work; he told me again that I didn't have to take the account if I didn't feel comfortable working with the man. I wasn't sure he had the authority to say that, but I appreciated the gesture. I glanced up and realized my break was over.

"I need to get back to work. Thanks again for lunch." I said as I got up from the table. He closed the dishes and put them in his insulated bag. I walked towards his door when he took my hand and turned me around. I realized he was going to kiss me again, so I quickly jetted out the door. I didn't want to get either of us in trouble with the boss.

Walking back to my desk I had a smile on my face. Sitting down I opened up my accounts and got to work. Time flew by and before I realized it, he was standing at my desk again. Austin cleared his throat, and I looked up about to ask what he needed when I realized everyone else had already left. We were the only ones left here. Glancing at the clock on my computer I realized it was six.

"Oh, I didn't realize how late it was. I'm sorry, were you waiting to lock up?" I asked him, biting my lip. I turned off my computer and stood up to put my purse on my arm when he groaned and pulled me into his arms. Placing one hand in my hair he wrapped the other one around my waist and pulled me in for a kiss. He nipped at my bottom lip and then sucked it into his mouth. I felt the kiss all the way to my clit. I wrapped my arms around him and held on as he plundered my mouth. Next thing I know he is walking me back to his office with his mouth still on mine. Austin slid his other arm down my back and sat on the couch pulling me into his lap. He started to kiss down my neck to my collarbone and across to the other side. It felt so good. He slid his hands up my blouse and popped my bra open. I gasped and leaned back to look into his eyes. They were heavy-lidded with desire. I looked for a minute then wrapped my arms around his neck and pulled him in for another kiss. Sucking his full lower lip into my mouth. Kissing Austin was quickly becoming one of my favorite things to do. He was about to raise my shirt up when we heard the front door open. We jumped apart and my eyes widened when I realized we were at work in his office with the door open. I hopped up and tried to refasten my bra quickly. Austin got up and walked out of his office pulling the door closed.

I heard him talking to Mr. Heath and took the opportunity to calm myself. Once I felt comfortable again, I started toward the door then I heard a door close, and Austin walked back into his office.

"I'm sorry, I should never have done that here. Mr. Heath is gone; he just forgot a file. He didn't even notice your purse sitting on your desk." He had my coat in his arms and helped me into it. Then he put my purse over my arm. Pulling his own coat on, he then led me out of his office and turned off the lights. We walked out together, and he walked me to my car. "I also told him you were attending the Christmas party with me on Friday. I hope that's okay with you." He said looking a little worried.

"That's fine, I just didn't want him to catch us in a compromising position." I was very flustered still.

"Well, I'm not at all sorry for kissing you. I have wanted to do that all day, but I will apologize for groping you at work. That was very unprofessional of me." He chuckled as he opened my car door for me. Leaning into me he pressed his lips to mine again. "Will you have dinner with me tomorrow? We can go out to eat. I want to keep seeing you and get to know you better."

"I'd like that. I need to get some grocery shopping done this evening on my way home. Let me know what time you want to pick me up tomorrow." I closed my car door and started the engine then watched as he climbed into his mustang. Taking a few calming breaths, I put the car in reverse and back out. I would just stop by the store and pick up a few things on the way home. Maybe some steaks and potatoes. I could offer to cook for him on Wednesday evening. That sounded like a great idea. I would have to decide what to wear and how far I wanted things to go.

One thing I knew for sure. Austin Wilson had the keys to my libido, and he knew exactly how to get the motor running. I can't wait to see him tomorrow. With that in mind I headed to the store.

8

G*ears*

There was an Irish pub that had great food near the Freedom/Liberty line, and I decided I would take her there tomorrow. It was slow on Tuesdays so we would be able to talk and enjoy each other's company. They had some of the best stew and it would be nice on a cold night. I was driving along when I heard my ring tone. I tapped my ear bud to answer it.

"Hey Axle." I answered briskly. I knew there may be some club business I would need to take care of so I could be free tomorrow evening.

"Hey, I know you just got off of work, but I need you to come by the clubhouse before you go home." Axle said rather than asked. I knew he wasn't much on niceties. He used to be more laid back when we were younger but when he lost his girl and his best friend moved to the next town over, he just closed up. Over the past year he had loosened up a bit but nothing like he used to be. I think it had to do with Annie, the Undertaker's wife was a sweetheart. All the guys loved her, and we all dotted on their little boy. Nobody thought he would ever have a family of his own after Lisa passed. When Annie came charging back into his life after their one-night stand, she changed him. He found something to live for again and he was so much happier. Whatever it was I would be there.

"See you in fifteen." I replied and hung up. I pulled up to the clubhouse fifteen minutes later, changed out of my regular coat and threw on my cut then went inside. I walked in to see all the guys at the large community table we had in the back.

"Hey Gears, you hungry?" Lillian asked as she came by the table. I nodded at her. She knew what I liked so I had no need to actually order anything. "All right be back in a minute."

"What's going on guys?" I asked, surprised to find them all here waiting. I sat down by Hawk who was looking super pissed. Axle rang his fingers through his hair and looked over at Hawk who was about to come out of his skin.

"Candy was killed last night, someone grabbed her outside the club when she got off her shift. The raped her and beat her to death. Bethann is beside herself. Candy was her baby sister, and those kids are her nephews. They don't have any other family, so she is going to be raising them now. She is going to have trouble managing a strip club and raising a couple of young kids. We need to figure out a different job for her and replace her at the club." Axle looked frustrated as hell, and I knew this triggered memories of Valkyrie.

"Well fuck, does anyone have any ideas? This time of year, most people are not hiring, and we live in a pretty small town." I said as Lillian put a plate in front of me. Sadly, I wasn't hungry anymore. I just murmured a thank you.

"Annie talked to her this morning. Apparently, Bethann lives in an efficiency apartment, and she has the kids sleeping on her bed while she crashes on the couch. We take care of our own around here. For now, she can stay at my place, and I'll crash here. That will give them somewhere to live rent free for now while we try to help her get back on her feet. She was doing fine but suddenly becoming a guardian to two children really throws a wrench in her lifestyle." Axle said staring blankly.

"No, I have three bedrooms at my place. Bethann can have one and the boys can have another. They are going to need a strong hand after something like this. I can also look after them and be sure she is taking care of herself. I don't like the idea that whoever attacked Candy could come after Bethann." Hawk said firmly. "I'll go over there after I we finish up here. Fang, can you take over the place until we can hire a replacement?"

"Sure man, whatever the club needs. You know that. Besides most of my work is contract anyway and I don't have anything in the works at the moment. I'll head over to the club and start talking to the employees and see if anyone has seen anything. You think it had anything to do with that asshole Richie?" Fang asked rubbing his beard checking his phone for any messages.

"I don't know but we need to find out as soon as we can. I need to head over to Bethann's so I can take her and the boys by their mom's trailer to get their things. I want to get them settled in before the weekend. The boys are out of daycare today and we are having her cremated. They didn't have any insurance or the money to pay for a funeral. I am paying for this; we will hold a small memorial for her here after Christmas so that the kids can have closure and any of her coworkers can pay their respects." Hawk got up and walked out. I knew he had been sweet on Bethann for a while, but I didn't realize how much he was into her. Hawk never had people in his house. The fact that he was about to take in a woman and her two orphaned nephews said a lot.

"Fang, come to my place and I'll go over the financials with you and the routine, so you know what to do. I'll give you my key and get Bethann's tomorrow. She won't be happy about taking charity, but she will get the fuck over it because she needs the help and it's for the boys." I got up and took my plate over to Lillian. "Lil, would you mind wrapping this up for me to take home."

She put it in a Styrofoam container for me and I headed to my place with Fang behind me. Walking in the front door I hung my cut up and put the food on the counter. I wasn't going to eat it, but I didn't want to hurt Lillian's feelings by throwing it out at the clubhouse.

"Give me a second to change and I'll be right out." I left Fang sitting at the table while I changed from my work clothes to an old pair of jeans and a long sleeve Henley. I shot off a text to Sophie to be sure she made it home okay then went back to the living room to go over what Fang needed to do at the club. We went over the nightly routine, what the girls made and what part they turned in of their tips. I wanted security beefed up a bit and the dancers walked to their cars. We were going to have a few prospects working security in and outside the club until we caught the bastards that killed Candy.

"Fang, I would prefer you make the deposit drop the next morning. Bring it back and lock it up at the clubhouse. I don't want anyone to be ambushed at the bank deposit drop. We will make biweekly deposits on different days. If you have any questions about financials call me, anything else in the club you can ask Hawk. He runs security there most nights." I glanced at my phone and saw that Sophie had responded. Smiling, I turned it back over.

"I heard you finally got that girl to go out with you. How is that working out?" Fang asked. He was very social and an all-around great guy. Don't get me wrong, he could bust your face up while smiling at you the whole time, but he had a way of making the ladies feel safe around him.

"Things seem to be going good so far. I'm hoping she will attend our club dinner with me. I did get her to agree to attend the work Christmas party with me on Friday." I smiled as I walked Fang to the door. "Be careful, watch your back"

Fang slapped me on the shoulder and gave me that mischievous grin of his. I knew I would be in for more ribbing later. He drove off and I locked up and went to heat up the burger. I tossed the fries because those are just nasty reheated. Looking down at my phone I read over the last couple of comments and responded.

Austin: You make it home okay babe?

Sophie: Yes, thanks for checking on me.

Austin: Sorry I didn't respond sooner, had some club business to handle right after work. Please be careful and don't be out after dark alone for now.

I didn't get a response right away, so I put down the phone and ate my burger with some chips and washed it down with a beer. What an awful night. I had only met Candy a few times, but she was a nice girl. She was just stripping because she had no education, and it was the best paying job she could find. I was going to worry about Sophie a lot more now. I finished eating and she had not answered yet. I looked at the clock and it was only nine pm. I decided to just call her.

"Hey Austin, everything okay with you?" she answered huskily. Her voice was so sexy and little raspy. I had to adjust myself.

"Hey baby, it's okay. Just some issues with safety at one of the businesses we are dealing with. I'm going to ask that you be extra vigilant when it comes to coming and going alone and locking up." I told her as I laid on my bed.

"I can do that. I was about to go to bed, what are you doing?" she asked me as I heard some rustling.

"Are you in your bed baby?" I asked her, imagining her in a soft t-shirt and some skimpy panties crawling between her sheets. I found myself gripping my cock at the thought.

"Yes, I'm glad you called so I could talk to you before I went to sleep. Hope I'll be able to sleep." She whispered softly.

"Anything I can do to help with that?" I asked her, wondering if she would be more comfortable with a little phone sex first. She moaned and I knew she was touching herself. "Are you touching yourself Sophie?"

"Yes, I am running my fingers down my chest and pinching my nipples. I am imagining it's you doing it." She let out a gasp and another moan.

"Are you pinching those soft full breasts?" I asked her as I stroked my hand up and down my hard cock. "I want you to run your hand down to your mound slowly, part yourself for me and find your clit. You with me?"

"Uh huh, now what?" she demanded. This girl was going to be a challenge.

"I want you to put your fingers in your mouth, get them nice and wet. Then run circles around your clit. Rub harder and faster while you imagine it's my tongue working you." I told her as I stroked faster. Damn I was so close to coming but I wanted her right there with me. I could hear her heavy breathing and I knew when she came because I heard her shout my name.

"Damn baby, you finish?" I asked her as I moaned and cum jetted all over my chest. I let a huge breath out.

"Yes, thank you. Sounds like you did the same." She said sounding proud of herself. "I'm about to fall asleep Austin." She yawned. "I'll see you in the morning. Night." She disconnected the call.

She wasn't the only one falling asleep. I reached over for some wipes to clean myself up and then turned out the light to go to sleep.

9

Sophie

It was early Tuesday morning when I woke up. My alarm had not gone off yet. I reached over to switch it off and stretched. That was one of the best nights sleep I have had in quite some time. I got up and went to turn on the coffee pot. Then headed back to my bathroom to shower and get ready for work. I wanted to look extra nice. I chose a knee length sweater dress in a dark blue with my knee length black boots. My hair I just blew dry with a big brush. Putting on the little makeup I usually wear, I slipped on my watch and went to drink my coffee.

I usually left for work about eight to be there by eight thirty. It was only seven forty-five. I pulled my laptop over to the table to check my email. Christmas was only a week and half away. I haven't spoken to my mother since I refused to come for dinner the other day. I knew she would be angry and ignore me for a couple of days. I was honestly fine with that; it was kind of peaceful. I loved my family, but I just got tired of being compared to my sister. I know she is my opposite. They want grandkids and she seems their only chance. I want kids but not until I'm ready. I looked at my phone and had a missed call from her. I sighed and hit call.

"Hey Mom." I said as I rinsed my coffee mug out and put it in the dishwasher. "How are you and dad doing?" I tried to be nice and diplomatic.

"Young lady, you do not hang up on me. I also did not appreciate you not showing up for dinner on Saturday night after I planned a dinner with you there." She sounded so put out I wanted to laugh. My mother always cooked too much food and she always had leftovers.

"I told you I was not coming. You were so insistent on my bringing a date, so you have an even number at the table. I told you I had no one to bring so I would not be coming so you have your even number. It's not my fault that you didn't believe me. I'm getting ready for work, so I need to go. I'll talk to you later." I hung up the phone and put it in my purse. It was time to go so I headed out.

Pulling in the parking lot I saw that Austin's mustang was already in his spot. I smiled and got out. Walking in I hung up my coat and purse on the stand behind my desk. I fired up my computer and checked work emails. I had a couple of clients coming in today and a few smaller deadlines for taxes. I was about to get up and go to the kitchen for coffee when I saw a cup set down in front of me just the way I like it. I glanced up and he winked at me. He nodded toward his office. I got up and followed him in there.

"Good morning, beautiful. How did you sleep?" he asked me as I blushed. Pulling his door closed he put his arms around me and kissed me. It was a sweet kiss. We knew we needed to behave at work. Stepping back he kissed my nose.

"I slept great, thanks." I told him, reaching for the door. "I have a lot of work to get through today. Would you like to come over for dinner later instead of going out?"

"I have to check with Axle and make sure there is nothing that I need to do for the club this evening, but it sounds good. What time should I be there?" he asked me with a smile on his face.

"I think six thirty would be good. If I'm home by five thirty I can get everything ready." I was standing by the door when I heard the front door open. "Just text me if it's an issue, I need to get to my desk before the vulture starts to circle." I rolled my eyes and walked to my desk. I sat down and sipped on the coffee he made me. Brittni was putting her purse away and I looked up to see her scowling at me. Huh, whatever. She needs to get over herself.

Work went by quickly. I had agreed to attend the company Christmas party with Austin this coming Friday, I needed to ask him about my parents' house next weekend. I had a sandwich at my desk from the deli around the corner. Austin did not come out of his office all day. I hoped he had brought some lunch. Around four thirty I got ready to leave and I knocked on his door. I heard him mumble for me to come in, so I pushed the door open. He was sitting at his desk focused on his computer.

"Are you okay? You haven't popped out of your office all day." I said as I walked over and sat on his desk and crossed my legs. He looked up at me and his eyes were suddenly hot with lust. "You work too hard; you need to knock off so you will be rested for dinner or rather after dinner." He closed his computer and moved it aside and then pulled me directly between his knees. Standing up he put both hands in my hair and pulled me in for a super-hot kiss. Nipping at my lip, I opened for him, and he had me pressed against him tightly. I heard a tap on his door, and he stepped back, gave me a wink and went to see who it was. I got off his desk and stood out of sight of the door. He opened the door and Brittni was there.

"Is there something you need before you leave Brittni?" Austin asked her clearly annoyed.

"Oh, I was going to see if you wanted to get dinner with me?" she said in a husky voice. I felt my nails curl into my palms. "We could grab something and take it back to my place."

"I'm seeing someone, and I wouldn't be interested if I wasn't. You should go home, you have been coming to work late this past week. I assume you just need to get more rest so that you can be on time." Austin was very firm with her. She looked around him and I knew she was looking for me. I decided to nip this in the butt. We don't have any fraternization rules here at our firm since it was so small. I walked up behind him and slipped my hand through his arm. He looked down at me in surprise.

"Brittni, it would be great if you would stop making a pass at my boyfriend. I'll see you tomorrow. Don't forget to get those accounts scheduled for review by the end of day tomorrow. We will be closed the week of Christmas, and I don't plan on taking any work home." I said pointedly to her then turned to Austin. I stood on my toes and kissed him on the cheek then whispered in his ear just loud enough she could hear me as well. "See you at my place honey."

I sashayed out of his office with Brittni's mouth hanging open. I heard her annoying shoes clicking after me.

"Ms. Boyd, you know you are not his type. He will get bored with you soon enough. All those bikers go through women like we go through shoes." Brittni said spitefully. I turned at the door and narrowed my eyes on her. She looked satisfied thinking she had scored a hit.

"Actually Brittni, you are not his type. He doesn't like vapid, narcissistic bitches. I promise you; I keep him plenty satisfied. Now run along, you wouldn't want to be written up again for being tardy." I glanced up and saw Austin smiling at me. Brittni stomped out and got in her car and left. I looked over at Austin and winked and left too. I need to get home and be sure to have dinner ready. I also wanted to make sure I had fresh sheets on my bed because I planned on seducing him tonight.

10

Gears

That woman! I couldn't stop smiling as I went to grab my coat and lock up the office. I got to my car and saw Sophie pulling away. She looked so gorgeous today in her short sweater dress and those boots. The way her short hair hit the top of her shoulders and her eyes sparkled. I loved that she didn't wear much makeup. She was a natural beauty. Brittni had been discreetly hitting on me for months and I tried to be polite but firm. Apparently, my girl had a jealous streak. It was very sexy.

I was heading home to change when my phone rang. It was Hawk, he was getting frustrated with Bethann's situation. He managed to get them moved into his place and the kids were taking the rest of the week off.

"Hey Hawk, what's up?" I asked him as I pulled up to the compound. I let myself in the gate and drove back to his place. He was sitting on his porch. Head in his hands. He looked exhausted.

"We told the kids about their mom, they both cried but then Cameron just kind of shut down on us. He won't talk at all. Joshua has been inconsolable. He won't let Bethie put him down. I don't know what the fuck to do." Hawk looked up at me with a frustrated expression and I felt bad for him. We knew he had a thing for Bethann but the fact that he was taking them into his home spoke volumes. Sean 'Hawk' McKay was a very private person. He didn't bring women to his house. I don't think I have ever been inside for that matter.

"Damn man, I know that had to be rough. All you can really do is be there for her. Maybe find a therapist for the kids to talk to. You are already doing a lot by taking them in and giving them a home and some stability." I scratched my beard as he looked up at me.

"I have never felt this way about a woman and to have two kids thrown into the mix. My Pa died when we were young, I barely remember him. I don't want them to grow up without a father figure in their lives. Bethann is so natural with them. I know it's really hard for her when she is grieving her sister at the same time, they are grieving the loss of the only parent they had." Hawk got up and stretched. "I'm going to go inside and fix dinner. Maybe we can coax them to eat just a bit. Thanks for stopping by."

"Anytime brother, we are always here for you. Tell Bethann hello for me. I'll stop by in a few days and check in on her. I'm heading over to Sophie's for dinner. Let me know if you need anything." I told him as I slapped him on the back and then left. I jerked my head at Gator who as usual had gate duty. He was the youngest fully patched member. There were several prospects around. We were trying to keep numbers down until we find out who was hurting women at our club. We couldn't take a chance of recruiting a traitor.

Driving to Sophie's I stopped by the grocery and picked up a bottle of wine along with a dozen roses. I was taught never to go to a lady's house empty handed. I needed to ask her about the Club Dinner after the Christmas Donation Run at the hospital. We had the work party on Friday night, the club dinner was Christmas evening at the clubhouse. I had secured her as my date for the office party, next I was going to ask about the club dinner.

Pulling up outside her place I parked by her window and walked up to the door and pushed the button to ring her apartment. I liked that it gave her an extra bit of security that she had this door as well as a door for her apartment. The door opened up and she was flushed and beautiful, she had changed out of the sweater dress into a long man's shirt and some leggings. She looked adorable. I handed her the flowers and the wine and walked inside with her. Holding her door open she walked inside and went straight to the kitchen to get a vase for her flowers. After setting them up she turned and pulled me down to kiss her.

"Thank you for the beautiful flowers." she said huskily licking her lips as she looked at me from under her long lashes. I loved that she was so natural. I leaned in and kissed her again pulling her into my body and holding her for a minute. She always smelled so good. Stepping back she glanced up at me and smiled.

"I'm glad you were able to come over. I made stew and some fresh bread to go with it. I always make too much because I like the leftovers. Would you like a glass of wine, or I have beer as well?" Sophie asked me as she started to open the bottle. I stepped over to her and took the bottle out of her hand gently and pointed to a chair.

"Baby, you sit down, and I'll fix our drinks and bring the food to the table." I told her pouring our wine and putting it on the table. I wasn't all that hungry anymore. I wanted to spread her out on the table and feast on her instead. She had the table set up with a Christmas candle in the middle and her Christmas plates out. I picked up our bowls one at a time and put stew in them and a couple of slices of bread on the side then took a seat close to her. "I forgot to tell you how lovely you looked today."

"Thanks, I had to change it was too warm to wear while I was cooking, and I didn't want to get red sauce on the cream sweater." She blushed as she glanced down.

"You look beautiful the way you are, but I don't care for you wearing another man's shirt." I told her feeling possessive. "That needs to go. I'll bring you one of mine to wear."

"Ok." she whispered as she continued to eat her dinner. When we were both finished, I took the plates to the kitchen and rinsed them off, placing them in the dishwasher then took our wine and headed to the living room.

I sat down and she stepped between my legs. Standing there looking down at me she started to undo the buttons on her shirt. Slowly she worked her way down to the last button and then crossed her arms to push the sleeves over her shoulders and she let it drop to the floor. She had taken off her leggings before standing in front of me so now she was there in nothing but a lacy thong. I was a bit dumbfounded since I wasn't sure we were headed for this tonight. I could tell when I had hesitated too long because she looked embarrassed and started to cover herself. That would not do at all.

"Don't cover yourself. I was just enjoying the vision in front of me. You are beautiful Soph. Every part of you is lush and gorgeous. Your body is made to cradle mine. Soft, welcoming and I'm betting wet." She gasped at my words and her eyes flew up to look at mine. I reached for her as I sat up and pulled her closer so that I could kiss her. I was going to show her exactly how desirable I found her. I reached up and put my hands on either side of her face and kissed her lips. First gently then I licked my lip along her bottom lip demanding entrance. She opened her mouth, and I delved inside. Tasting her sweetness and the wine I kissed and swirled our tongues mating our mouths like I planned to mate our bodies. I kissed my way to her ear and whispered. "If you want to stop, tell me now." She shook her head and tilted it giving me better access. I kissed my way down her neck to her breasts, they were full and lush with large areolas and pink nipples. When I grabbed a handful of one and sucked into my mouth, she moaned and arched her back into me. My girl was sensitive, so I did the same with the other side. Alternating between them and nipping lightly to see what got the most reaction from her. She liked a little rough play. Good to know, I wanted to finish my journey but in her bed. I stood up and slid my arms down her butt and picked her up as she wrapped her legs around my waist. I remembered where she said her room was, so I carried her to her bed as she quickly unbuttoned my shirt. I wasn't as cut as a lot of the guys, but I knew I was in good shape. She slid it over my shoulders, and I set her on the edge of the bed as it fell to the floor. I knelt in front of her and pulled the lacy thong down her shapely legs. I put it to my nose and smelled her arousal. She swallowed hard when she saw me do it. I pocketed the panties and then bent to my dessert. She was shaved smoothly and had dew glistening on her lips from her arousal. I leaned in and swiped my tongue through her folds. She was sweet, tangy and I wanted more. I held her legs open as I dipped my tongue into her, I felt her clinch. Sucking her labia into my mouth she moaned. I rotated back and forth then started to flick my tongue on her click. I slipped a finger inside her as I did this then a second. I could feel her tightening around my fingers and I couldn't wait to feel that around my cock. I started to move my fingers faster pumping into her and then I nipped her clit, and she went off like a rocket. Screaming my name and holding onto my head. Looking up at her I licked my lips and stood up to remove the rest of my clothes. She started to crawl across the bed to reach for my cock when I stopped her shaking my head.

"Baby, I am too close, and I want to come inside of you not in your hand. Let me grab a condom." After ensuring that I was covered I pulled her down the bed with her hips. Leaning over and lining myself up with her entrance I slid in slowly watching the expression on her face as I filled her. I didn't let her get a good look at me because while I was not as bulky in the muscle department, I was very well endowed, and women had a tendency to tense up when they saw me. I wanted her to relax. I wrapped her legs around my waist and bent to kiss her lips. She was a vision laid out, body flushed, and eyes glazed. I wanted to burn that image into my brain. We moved together, finding a rhythm that suited us both and I could tell she needed something else. I reached between us and began to rub circles around her clit while I picked up my pace thrusting in and out of her. Suddenly her entire body tensed up and she was coming all over my cock. I could feel the tight flutters of her walls clenching around me. I couldn't hold back and then I came with her. When the aftershocks wore off, I slid out of her and went to dispose of the condom. I walked back into the bedroom with a warm damp cloth to clean her up. I also figured it would soothe the soreness. Placing the cloth over her, I lay down beside her pulling her into my arms.

"That was amazing. Damn Sophie, you are a firecracker." I told her as I kissed her head. She giggled into my chest, and I decided that was my favorite sound and it would be my goal to make her do that often. She started to get up and I tightened my hold on her. "Where are you going?"

"I need to use the restroom and I'm thirsty." She blushed as she headed to the bathroom. I watched her snag my dress shirt off the floor and slide it on. She glanced back at me and winked.

11

Sophie

OMG: OMG, OMG I just had sex with Austin Wilson. Holy Shit. It was amazing and who knew the man was so skilled with his tongue. My pussy clenches just thinking about what he did. I quickly use the restroom and wash myself. I decided not to put on any underwear and see if he is planning to sleep over. I ran the brush through my hair and flipped it to make it not look too perfect. I walk back in the room to see him watching me. He has his underwear on and is sitting on the edge of the bed.

I bet he is about to bolt. Suddenly I feel very self-conscious of being in his shirt and only his shirt. I feel like I need clothes as a security blanket. He must have seen something on my face because he got up and walked over to me. Pulling me into his arms he breathes in my scent and then leans back and kisses me.

"I don't know what you are thinking but I'm pretty sure it's not anything close to what I am." He says to me as I bite my lip and look down. "No, look at me Sophie. I would like to spend the night, but I don't want to impose or make assumptions."

My eyes shot up to his at his comment. I swallow hard and think about how nice it would be to go to sleep in his arms and wake up there. I nodded because I couldn't speak past the lump in my throat. He started to pull away and I tightened my hold on him.

"Please stay. I would like that." I said as I laid my head down on his chest. I felt the tension leave his body. He walked me back to the bed and pulled back the covers to tuck me in. "Did you change your mind?"

"No baby, I packed a bag to keep in the car in case I was lucky enough to get to stay with you one night. I don't want to have to leave super early to go home and change. I just need to run out to my car and grab the bag." He kissed me and pulled his pants on and put on his jacket.

I watched as he left the room and then laid my head back on the pillow and thought about his mouth on my body. I slid my hand slowly down to my breasts pinched them and then slid my hand down to my clit. How in the world was I all turned on again already. I licked my lips and started to rub circles around it, I was moaning and writhing on the bed when Austin walked back in.

"Hey babe, would you........." he dropped his bag as he realized what I was doing. I jerked my hand back when I realized he was standing there. "Oh no, don't stop now. You look so hot."

He took his clothes back off and prowled over to the bed. Austin never took his eyes off of me as he stripped and then climbed up beside me. Having him watch me touch myself was so intense. He leaned down and sucked on my breast while I worked my clit harder. I was almost there when he looked me in the eyes.

"Come for me baby, let me see your pleasure." His voice and command sent me over the edge. My body tensed up and then I tipped over. He moved between my legs and lapped me up. "You taste so good

Soph." he climbed up my body and thrust inside me then he flipped us to put me on top.

"Oh, I'm too heavy." I said as he smacked my ass hard and frowned. He shook his head and pulled me down for a kiss.

"Don't insult my girl like that again or I'll have to put you over my knee. You are perfect. Now move, I want to see you come again before we get some sleep." He demanded as he held my hips and helped me ride him. I had never done this before. He was so much deeper in this position, and it felt amazing. I rolled my hips, then raised and lowered my body on him squeezing him with my inner muscles. He was getting close and so was I. Suddenly he flipped me over and took me from behind. He pounded into me fast and hard holding me around the waist. He bit my neck, and I was coming again. It felt like an ongoing orgasm that wouldn't stop. When we both finished, he pulled out gently and grabbed some wipes from the side of the bed to clean me up with. Then he pulled me into his body and covered us up.

"Go to sleep baby, we have to get up and go to work tomorrow." He kissed my head and wrapped his arms around me. I was asleep in minutes.

My horrible alarm went off at six as usual. I rolled over and jumped when I saw Austin laying beside me. I forgot for a moment that he stayed over. Thinking about what we did last night I blushed. How was I going to face him at work all day?

"I need to take a shower" I mumbled as I tried to get out of bed. Austin had other ideas though. He pulled me under him and slipped back inside me. I was still wet, and it was like he belonged there. He leaned down to kiss me as he gently made love to me. We matched a slow, leisurely rhythm that was so different from last night I almost had tears in my eyes. He touched my face as he looked at me. Reaching between our bodies he found my clit and gave a small pinch, and I exploded all over him. I swear he has a handbook to my body. He pulled away from me and got up.

"Wait here a minute." Austin walked toward the bathroom. I heard the shower come on and then he came back and picked me up and took me to shower with him. "We can shower together. I'll wash your hair for you." He told me as he set me on my feet in the shower and grabbed the shampoo. After I got my hair wet, he lathered some in and massaged my scalp before rinsing out the shampoo. After repeating that process, he conditioned it and then started to wash my body. I got some body wash and started on his at the same time. He was lean but muscled, you could tell he took care of his body. I never knew what he was hiding under the suits. Yummy. We rinsed the soap off, and he got out to get us both towels to dry off. I wrapped my towel around my body as I dried off. Sitting at my vanity, I picked up my brush and blow dryer to fix my hair. Austin had dried off and was dressed already in his usual slacks, dress shirt and tie. When I finished with my hair I put on my makeup and got up to get dressed. I chose a pair of tights and a long sheath style dress. Slipping on some low-heeled pumps I put on my sapphire studs and a matching necklace, spritzed on some body spray that smelled like coconut and then went to get some coffee.

"You look beautiful baby. I fixed you some toast and coffee." Austin placed it down at the table and pulled out my chair. I glanced at the clock, and we still had fifteen minutes before we had to leave.

"Thank you." I took a drink of my coffee and noticed it was fixed exactly how I liked. I looked up at him surprised.

"I have been paying attention for a long time. You just didn't realize it." He winked at me and took a drink of his coffee. "I would have made a bigger breakfast, but we have the end of year meeting today and Lee is having breakfast catered in."

"Oh, I almost forgot about that. I have all my accounts up to date and ready though." Chewing on my lips nervously I looked up at him. He was finishing his toast and coffee while watching me. I wanted to ask him about my family dinner.

"What's on your mind baby?" he asked me as he reached for my hand. "You can tell me anything. I didn't expect our relationship to move this fast, but I have no complaints."

"My sister is getting married on Valentine's Day and so her fiancé comes to all the dinners and family events we have. My mother has been pressuring me to bring someone with me to Christmas dinner. I kept telling her I wasn't seeing anyone and didn't want to bring a stranger but...." I hesitated and looked at him. Austin smiled at me.

"Baby, I would love to go with you to their home for dinner. I also have a family dinner of sorts Christmas weekend. I would like you to come to mine as well." He suggested with his eyebrow raised in question. I relaxed at that moment and nodded.

"I would love to go to your Christmas dinner as well. They aren't around the same time I hope." I said frowning. "We eat around three and then open gifts."

"The club delivers toys to the Childrens' hospital after lunch. We have our Christmas dinner late around eight, I'll be helping with that and then I'll stop and pick you up." He told me as he got up and reached for my coat to help me with it. Then he slipped his on so we could leave.

"Do you want to ride together? We could grab dinner after work." Austin suggested. "We need to talk to Mr. Heath as well, but there are some things I need to tell you and I want you to hear them from me."

I looked at him a little startled. I hated that there might be more secrets between us. Frowning I got into his car as he opened the door. He closed it and got in on his side.

"What are you keeping from me?" I asked him in a whisper. He slips my hand in his and kisses the back of it. I knew I was already falling for him. He rubbed the back of my hand nervously.

"First let me tell you that nobody knows what I am about to tell you except Lee. It's not a big secret from you specifically. This still needs to be kept quiet, but being as we are in a relationship you need to know." He squeezed my hand. "I am a silent partner with Lee in the company. I own half of it. I just don't want managerial responsibilities. I prefer to do my work and be left alone to handle club business. We also didn't want anyone thinking that the firm was a front for anything. It isn't." He risked a glance over at me.

I stared at him a little dumbfounded and tried to wrap my head around the fact that I was sleeping with my boss. My face was fire engine red, and I couldn't string a sentence together to save my life.

12

Austin 'Gears'

I was really nervous; she had not said anything since I dropped the bomb about owning half the company. She didn't let go of my hand, but she was really quiet. I didn't want to ruin things between us. I really liked her and wanted to explore this thing we had between us. I kept glancing over at her and she was just staring blankly out the window.

"Baby, are you mad at me?" I looked over at her as I asked. She raised her eyes to mine and then glanced back out the window. Oh boy. "I'm sorry I didn't tell you sooner. I never had any intention of anyone knowing but being as I want to see where this goes with us and I care about you, I felt you should know. Especially since you work with me."

"Austin, you're my boss. How am I supposed to not worry about what people will think." she asked me as she bit her lip. Damn, every time she did that, I wanted to kiss her.

"Baby, nobody else knows. This is not common knowledge, and I don't want it to be. I invested money and I work on my own accounts, but I don't do any supervisory roles. Technically Lee is your boss and that's how it stays. You don't answer to, me at work. As far as you are concerned, I'm your boyfriend and a coworker." We pulled into the parking lot, and I turned off my car. "Please don't be angry or let this come between us."

She looked at me with her eyes wide as saucers and repeated. "Boyfriend?" I got kind of tickled that she got stuck on that part of the sentence.

"Well, I hope you consider me your boyfriend since I was balls deep in your sweet body several times last night. I certainly consider you my girlfriend at this point." I smiled at her, leaned over and kissed her. I didn't care that we were in the parking lot, and I didn't care who saw us. Sophie Boyd was mine.

"Well okay." She said as I leaned back. I got out of the car and came around to open her door. I helped her out and put my arm around her waist. As we turned toward the building we were met by Brittni's glare. She suddenly smirked and went inside. "Ugh, she looks like she wants to stir up trouble."

"She doesn't have a leg to stand on, we have no fraternization rules, and we are disclosing our relationship to Lee this morning. Besides it's not like she can get us fired either. If nothing else, she is close to being out on her rude ass. I'm sick of her attitude." I slipped my hand around hers lacing our fingers and we walked into the building. I left Sophie at her desk while I walked to Lee's office whistling. I heard Sophie giggle and I turned to wink at her as I knocked on Lee's door. I opened it and walked inside to see him sitting at his desk looking frustrated.

"What's wrong Lee?" I asked him as I sat down on the chair in front of his desk. "You look like shit man."

"Thanks, you look like the cat who ate the canary." He mumbled and cursed his phone going off again. Reaching over, he turned it off and then looked at me, eyes narrowed. "You must have finally made headway with Ms. Boyd."

"Yes, Sophie and I are together. She knows about our arrangement and won't say anything. She was actually relieved to know I was not her direct supervisor." I crossed my leg over my knee and focused on my partner. "You seem really stressed out. I have looked over the books, so I know it's not work related. What's going on?"

"Wife is pregnant, we found out today it's going to be twins." He grinned and shook his head. "Twins, hell I barely have time for us lately."

"I can take a bigger role here if you need me to, or we can look into hiring someone else after the first of the year. Family comes first." I told him, thinking that if it was Sophie, I would want to put her first. "Try not to think about it too hard. We are going to be closed next week for Christmas. We will brainstorm after Christmas and figure it out. The Christmas party is the day after tomorrow, all the accounts are settled for the year. Why don't you go home and spend time with Ella?"

"Are you sure?" he said thinking about it. "That would make her really happy. She wants to wait to share the news at Christmas." He stood up and put his coat on. "Are we doing bonuses at the party as usual?"

"Yes, I already cut the checks and have them in the gift bags with their grocery certificates. See you at the party." I told him as I got up and walked out with him.

Walking out the door he didn't spare a glance at anyone. I winked at Sophie who smiled back at me. I closed the door to my office and sat down to get some paperwork finished up and close out my accounts for the year. I also checked to see that Sophie had finished hers. She not only finished but looked like she had a head start on the next quarter. My phone beeped and I looked to see a text from Hawk letting me know that Bethann and the boys would be at Christmas dinner at the clubhouse. She was going to help Lillian cook Christmas dinner. Fury and Axle would be frying turkeys, the ladies were handing the sides and desserts. Bear was coming and bringing his family. It had been a while since he had attended a club family meal. We missed him and were really glad that he and Axle had mended fences. I messaged back that Sophie would be attending with me. Looking up I noticed it was past lunch, we were supposed to have had a meeting and since Lee went home early, we didn't have it. I was about to go check on Sophie when I heard a tap on my door. I opened it to see her standing there with two plates in her hand. I took them and gestured for her to come in then locked the door.

"I figured you had not eaten, and Mr. Heath emailed us to say that he was postponing the meeting until after Christmas and that breakfast was in the kitchen. When you didn't come out, I decided to make you a plate." She reached into my mini-fridge and pulled out a couple of bottles of water and sat down at my small table. I leaned over and kissed her softly.

"Thanks baby, I realized about five minutes ago that we didn't have the meeting and you may be hungry." I smiled as I sat down with her and took a bite of the warmed-up casserole. "This is really good."

"Mr. Heath ordered a few of the breakfast quiches from the market, they are well insulated, so they stayed warm." She told me as she devoured hers. "I was starving too, someone kept me up late last night."

I laughed out loud at her comment. She was feeling sassy this morning and I loved it. We finished our food in silence and then I took the dishes and tossed them in the trash.

"Do you have any plans for this evening?" I asked her as she got up to leave. She wrinkled her cute little nose and sighed.

"I need to go by my parents' house and make amends with my mother. I don't want it to be super awkward Christmas, so I need to do a little damage control." She groaned, closing her eyes. I stood up and put my arms around her. She wrapped her arms around my waist and laid her head on my chest. Then she leaned back to look up at me and pulled on my tie. I let her pull me down for another kiss. "Do you mind dropping me off at home after work?"

"Of course not baby, will you call me when you get back home?" I asked her, I didn't want to crowd her. "I just want to know that you got home safely."

"I can do that, let's get back to work so we can leave on time today." She said as she went back to her desk. I saw Brittni jump up from Sophie's desk and walk quickly back to hers.

"Sophie, just a minute. I need to check something." I pulled her away from her desk and sat down. I looked through the most recently accessed systems and saw where Brittni was trying to sabotage her work. She was messing with the figures to try and get Sophie into trouble. Her mistake was not knowing that I had already checked over her work not even an hour ago. I screenshot what was done and sent it to my own email before correcting the account back the way it was. Then I sent Sophie an email from my phone and left her screen open to her email so she would see it immediately. I stood up and gestured for her to sit down. Brittni was studiously not looking at us. I waited for Sophie to finish reading the email and then went to my office. I messaged Lee letting him know what happened and that we would be terminating her employment. I decided to give them the rest of the week off so that she would not have the opportunity to mess with any more of Sophie's work. I printed out the proof and then pulled the security footage of the front office area and sent the clips of Brittni at Sophie's desk to my email. I wanted all the proof ready. I wrote up her separation notice and termination papers. I printed everything and placed it in a file in my desk before locking that drawer. I sent the email next telling them to go home and we would see them at the Christmas party.

13

Sophie

I was shaking with rage when I read the email Austin had discreetly sent to me while I was standing there. It took everything in my power to hold my temper. I knew he wanted to do this in a way that kept his secret. I was glad that I would get to leave early and deal with my mother though. I locked all my files and then heard my email alert letting me know that we were closing early for the holiday and could go home. I closed down my computer and waited for Brittni to leave. She got up with a smug look on her face and walked out.

Snagging my purse out of the bottom drawer, I put my coat on and waited for Austin to come out of his office. He walked out a minute later, turning off the lights and walked me out. After locking everything up he led me to the car and helped me in. After he was in the car, he looked at me and his eyes were almost black with rage.

"I can't believe that bitch thought she was going to sabotage you and get you fired." He was seething. I reached over and took his hand.

"How did you know?" I asked him confused. "We were both in your office."

"I saw her get up when you were walking out of my office. I also check everyone's work periodically to be sure there are no issues. I had just finished checking over your accounts about an hour before you came in with the food. I knew she was up to something. I sent everything to my email and corrected what she changed. She will be fired at the Christmas party. All of the proof and paperwork are printed and locked in my desk as well as emailed to Lee's personal email as well as the company email." Austin reached out and pulled me to him for a searing kiss, then drove me home.

We pulled up outside my place so I could get my car. Austin left his car running. "Babe, give me your keys and you sit in here in the warm car." I watched him get out and get into my car to crank it. He sat there for a few minutes until he seemed satisfied and then got out and opened the door for me.

"Now your car is warm. Call me when you get home baby, let me know how it went." He said as he pulled me close and kissed me again. "I am getting addicted to your taste Soph." With another kiss on the forehead, he held the door while I got in my car then he closed it and waited for me to pull out. I smiled all the way to my parents' place.

I pulled up to the house I grew up in and put my head down for a minute. I hated to fight with my mother, but she had always favored my younger sister. It was always Pammy this and Pammy that. Now that Pamela was getting married, she thought I needed to be as well. I know she didn't mean to hurt me, but she just didn't think before speaking and it hurt. I took my purse and got out of the car, walking to the door. My dad was always tinkering in the garage, he liked to build things. He saw me first and walked over to hug me.

"Hey baby girl, why aren't you at work?" he asked as he put an arm around me and pulled me to his side. "You didn't get yourself fired, did you?" He winked at me. I knew he was teasing.

"No Papa, I didn't get fired. We were all caught up and they decided to give us a couple of extra days of our holiday. Is Mother inside?" I asked him. He smirked at me. He knew our relationship was tumultuous as best sometimes. I guess it balanced out though because I had always been daddy's girl.

"Your mother is inside cooking dinner. Apparently, Pamela and Jamie are joining us. I sure would enjoy a dinner with just the four of us one more time and I don't mean Jamie." Papa snorted in frustration and went back to the garage. I went in through the garage door and saw my mother standing in front of the stove putting a roast back in the oven. She must have been adding the vegetables mid-cooking. She looked up at me as I walked in. My mother was still a lovely woman, she was around my height with dirty blonde hair and bright blue eyes. I had my dad's hazel eyes. Pamela looked like our mother. She had long blonde hair and blue eyes. She also didn't carry around the extra weight I did. It was so unfair.

"Hey Mom, something smells good." I said trying to make amends. She looked at me for a minute and smiled.

"You look lovely sweetheart. Why are you off so early today?" she asked with a little frown. So, we were doing this. She was going to ignore my hanging up if meant I ignored her trying to guilt me into a date.

"We were finished with the year-end accounts and they decided to add a couple days off to our holiday vacation." I said as I sat at the counter. "Mom, I'm sorry that I hung up on you the other day."

"I'm sorry too, I shouldn't have made it sound like I didn't want you to come if it was just you. That was wrong. Your father was very angry with me." She looked near to tears. I got up and gave her a hug.

"If it will make you feel better, I have a boyfriend now." I said quietly as she hugged me back. She pulled away and looked at my face for a minute. "It's a recent thing. I work with him, and I always thought he was handsome, but I misjudged him at first. He is coming with me to Christmas dinner."

"That's wonderful Sophie, we look forward to meeting him. Actually, I always cook way too much. If you are both available for dinner this evening, I would love to meet him. Maybe break the ice before Christmas." She bit her lip and I laughed to myself as I realized she is where I got the habit from. "I mean if you want to come alone tonight, I'd love to have you here but if you want to bring him along that is good too."

I knew she felt bad about our conversation earlier in the week and she was trying. I guess I could text Austin and see. I pulled out my phone and sent him a quick text.

Sophie: Made up with Mom, she invited us for dinner tonight.

Austin: That's great love, what time?

"What time do you want him here?" I asked her, holding my phone. She smiled and said, "six would be good".

Sophie: six o'clock. Do you want to meet me here or ride together?

Austin: You are already there. Why don't you visit, and I'll just meet you there at six.

Sophie: okay I will see you in a bit.

Austin: See you soon baby.

I put my phone down smiling and her a gasp. I glanced up and my mother was smiling at me.

"What is it?" I asked her as she hugged me again.

"I don't remember ever seeing you this happy. You are absolutely glowing from just a little text." She smiled as she closed the oven door and set her timer. I remembered that he would need to the address, so

I shot off a quick text to him with that and then put my phone in my purse. Since I came from work, I knew that I looked nice.

"Austin will be here at six, he suggested I stay and visit. Anything new on the wedding front?" I asked, trying to sound interested. I just wasn't into the whole big wedding thing. If I get married, I want something low key.

"Everything is going great. We will be having fittings right after Christmas. That way if anything maybe we will have to have the dresses taken in just a bit before the wedding." She said as she pulled out a magazine and put it in front of me. "Pammy picked out a lovely eggplant color for the bridesmaid's dresses. It will be a great color on you. They are also simple and wearable after the wedding. I suggested she do this so it would be more practical for those purchasing the dress."

I pulled the magazine over and looked at the dress. It was an A-line sheath style dress with thick straps instead of spaghetti straps. It was actually very attractive and would be flattering even with my full figure. I breathed a sigh of relief.

"I would have thought she would go with red since it is on Valentine's Day." I said surprised. Mom shook her head.

"Pamela's best friend Krissy, suggested the red and Pam said no that it was not a good color for you, and she would not pick something that her sister would be uncomfortable wearing." She smiled at me, and my eyes teared up a little.

"Really?" I said huskily, trying not to cry. I did not want puffy eyes when Austin got here. "I'll thank her when she gets here and tell her how much I love what she picked out."

"That would be nice, the two of you were close when you were younger. It would be nice if you could be friendly again." My mother said pointedly. I don't think she realized that it was her constant comparison of us that drove the wedge. I didn't like to be compared to my sister nonstop and always coming up lacking. I was size fourteen, I had been a size fourteen since high school. Pamela wore a size six on her biggest day. We were built completely differently. I could not help it. I could not eat for a week and would be lucky to lose two pounds. She could eat all day every day and not gain anything. It was just a fact of life. Most of the time I didn't think about it but sometimes it was so frustrating.

"I'll try Mom. I promise." I told her. "Let's plan our Christmas dinner and you can let me know what I need to bring. I'm also supposed to have dinner with Austin's family Christmas night. I'd like to take something with me."

"That would be lovely dear." She said as she pulled out her cookbook. We poured over that for a few hours making our choices. I chose to make a sweet potato casserole to take to the MC clubhouse dinner. I didn't tell my mom that it was his MC family I was referring to. No need to disrupt a nice visit.

14

Austin 'Gears'

I was meeting her family tonight. This sure has moved quickly I thought to myself as I pulled up at the garage. I wanted to check on Undertaker, Annie and Mattie. It was still funny to see Taker so whipped. I chuckled as I walked inside, Fury was bent over an engine and Axle was doing an oil change. I didn't see Annie or Taker anywhere.

"Hey guys, where's Taker and Annie?" I asked looking around. I would see them at Christmas dinner, but I tried to keep up with everyone and be more social. Fury grunted at me, no surprise there. He wasn't the most social person and could be downright nasty sometimes.

"Annie was feeling queasy, so Undertaker took her home. I bet she's knocked up again." Axle smirked as he went back to what he was doing. I knew he was laughing because Taker thought he would never have kids and then he knocked Annie up the first time they were together. They were always glued to each other. I shook my head and smiled.

"I guess we will know soon enough. I have some chicken soup and crackers at my place. I'll swing by and drop some off for her." I said as I looked in the kitchen for a ginger ale. We kept that stuff stocked up when she was pregnant with Mattie. Sure enough, there were a couple of two liters beside the fridge. I grabbed one and headed to my place. I was still dressed nicely from work, so I decided not to change clothes. I went to the cabinet and pulled out a box of saltine crackers and a couple cans of chicken broth to take to Annie. I had plenty of time for a quick visit before I went to the Boyd's house for dinner.

Undertaker lived within walking distance of my house on the compound, so I just put my coat on and walked over. I knocked on the door and listened to Mattie wailing. Oh boy, someone was not happy. A minute later a very frazzled looking Undertaker opened the door. He looked at me and I held out the bag. His eyes narrowed as he looked at the contents and then his face just relaxed.

"Oh man, thank you. Annie has been feeling sick all day, Mattie wouldn't take a nap and I'm about to climb the walls. I was about to run out and get this stuff for her, but I didn't want to leave her alone with the baby while she was running back and forth to the bathroom." He took the bag, and I followed him inside. While he went to fix her a drink and take her some crackers, I went and picked up Mattie. The poor guy looked exhausted, and his little eyes were all puffy. I walked into the kitchen with him on my hip and grabbed one of the bottles Annie kept prepped for him. After a quick heat in the microwave, I shook it and checked the temperature on my wrist the way she showed me. Mattie had calmed down some and laid his head on my shoulder with his thumb in his mouth. I gently pried it out and replaced it with the bottle. Walking around feeding him I thought that maybe I would have this one day. I knew when he had finally fallen asleep because I felt him slump against me. Quietly I walked into his nursery and put him to bed. I left on his nightlight and turned on his little noise maker. After covering him up I pulled the door almost closed and walked back into the living area to see Annie in Undertakers' lap sipping on some ginger ale.

"Hey Gears, where's Mattie?" she asked me softly. "I noticed he finally stopped crying."

"I fed him a bottle, he's asleep. I just put him to bed. I think he could feel the tension and was likely reacting to you feeling bad." I told her as I leaned down and kissed her forehead. Taker growled at me.

"Oh hush, you big neanderthal. You know you're the only man I want." She reprimanded her old man and I just laughed. Nobody talked to the ex-prez like that except for her. He was known for making grown men wet themselves. Annie had his wrapped firmly around her little finger.

"I have dinner plans, but I heard you were feeling bad, so I brought you some ginger ale, crackers and soup. I hope you are feeling better soon." I told her as I looked at her old man watching her. "Do I need to send one of the guys out for a pregnancy test?"

Annie's eyes almost popped out of her head, and I swear Taker blanched at the thought. They looked at each other and started laughing.

"Oh shit, you think?" Annie said as she started to consider the idea. "What am I gonna do with two toddlers at once."

"I'm calling Doc, I'm sure he has some or he can just take a blood sample and check that way. He can also give you a checkup." Undertaker grumbled as he shot a text to our brother. "Thanks for bringing that stuff by. I'll call you later."

"I'm heading over to Sophie's parents for dinner so if you could just send a text if you need anything, I'll check it periodically." I told them as I headed for the door. "She is coming to Christmas dinner at the clubhouse."

"That's great, we can't wait to meet her." Annie said smiling brightly. All the guys loved her she was such a sweetheart. "I sure could use another female around here."

"Goodnight." I said, making a quick exit. I looked at my watch and saw that I had just enough time to stop and pick up some flowers before I went to dinner. I climbed into my mustang and headed to the florist.

I was hoping to make a good impression on her parents but at the same time I was going to be ready to defend my girl. Sophie had told me a little bit about their family dynamic, and it seemed she gets the short end of the stick quite often. I was going to make it my mission to spoil her rotten. I walked inside the shop and spotted Mira, she had been running this shop since her mother retired. I went to school with her.

"Hey Austin, what can I help you with?" Mira asked as she finished an arrangement she was working on. I waited for her to put it in the cooler.

"I would actually like to get a Christmas cactus and then some of the pink sweetheart roses in a bouquet." I said thinking there was no way I was not getting my girl flowers. "I'm meeting my girl's parents tonight."

"I'm so happy for you. So, I am assuming the cactus is for the mother and roses are for your lady?" she inquired. I nodded as I looked around. "I'll have that ready in just a minute."

Mira rang me up and I left with the flowers. I ran into the liquor store and picked up a bottle of wine. I chose a sweet red that was Sophie's favorite, then headed over to her parent's house.

Pulling up I took notice of the house. It was a nice two-story colonial house with some lovely flower boxes on the side. It was decorated for Christmas with lights all over and a couple of skinny trees lining the door. Very charming, I thought as I got out and walked to the door. Thankfully the cactus was in a carrying container with a handle. I ring the doorbell and step back a bit. The door flies open, and I see Sophie in her stocking feet smiling at me with a glass of wine in her hand. I smirked and raised my eyebrow at her. She giggles and it is the best sound ever.

"Hi baby, looks like you got started already." I told her as I handed her the roses. She beams and stands on her tiptoes to kiss me. "I have some wine and this plant for your mother."

About that time, I see a lady in her mid-forties walking toward the door. Blonde hair in a cute short hair style with blue eyes, she is smiling as she reaches out to shake my hand.

"I'm Julie Boyd and you must be Austin. It's a pleasure to meet you, come on in." she says as she gestures for me to come inside and closes the door. "Pamela and Jamie will be here shortly, they got stuck in traffic. Would you like a glass of wine."

"That sounds nice, and these are for you." I handed her the cactus and the wine. She beams at me so I'm assuming I made a good choice. "My mama always loved flowers and I know Sophie does too."

"Thank you so much, I love Christmas' cactus. Let me take your jacket and you can get settled. Tom is getting cleaned up for dinner." She places the wine on the counter and puts the cactus on the mantle. "Sophie and I have been planning Christmas dinner. She is looking forward to meeting your family."

I looked over and Sophie's eyes got wide, and she shook her head. Ah, she had not told her mother that I was part of the local MC. I knew she was not ashamed, but they would find out eventually. I winked at her. We went into the den and sat on the couch. Sophie sat close to me, and I placed my arm around her. We were chatting and I saw a tall well-built man come into the room. I stood up to shake her father's hand.

"I'm Thomas Boyd, Sophie's father." Her dad said as he shook my hand with a nice firm grip. "Sophie was telling me about you earlier. Austin, correct?"

"Yes sir, my name is Austin Wilson. I work with Sophie." I said as I noted that he was sizing me up. I knew that Sophie was his first born and they were very close. I respected that. "Sophie told me you like to build things."

"Love to work with wood, I'd be glad to show you my shop sometime." He looked around. "Where are James and Pamela?"

I heard the door close right then and a couple came into the room. A woman with long blonde hair, blue eyes and very thin followed by a very blonde man with blue eyes as well. He looked like he had just stepped off a tennis court and I had to try hard not to snicker out loud. The woman I'm assuming was her sister looked at me and seemed to be surprised.

"We are here. I'm sorry we were late." Pamela said as she took off her coat to hand up. That was already a point against him. He should have helped her with that.

"It's my fault Mr. Boyd, I had to take a call from my boss, and he was quite long winded." Jamie said as he hung his coat up and then led her into the room. "Dinner smells delicious."

I noticed the sour look on Thomas Boyd's face as he narrowed his eyes on the man. He must not care for him much. Hopefully I would fare better with him.

15

Sophie

I smiled to myself at the look on my dad's face. He had not warmed up to Jamie yet, hence the insistence on calling him James. I think he didn't like the fact that he was always over here eating, and he never brought anything or offered to. He also acted like it was Pamela's place to wait on him. I didn't know what she saw in him. I mean sure he was nice looking, at least until he opened his mouth. Ugh, well that was her problem.

"Sophie, you look nice today." Pamela said as she gave me a one arm hug. I loved my sister, but she could be so disingenuous sometimes. I looked at her and as usual she was wearing a fancy dress and heels. Honestly how she could walk in those things all the time baffled me. I had a few glasses of wine already, so I was going to be generous and accept the compliment.

"Thank you, so do you. Is that a new dress?" I asked her not really caring one way or another. She preened so I knew I had guessed correctly.

"Yes, thank you. I found it online at Neiman-Marcus. It was on sale for $200." I choked on my wine and looked at her horrified. "Are you okay? Maybe you should switch to water."

Austin's hand tightened slightly on my back when she said that. He was very protective of me.

"You know they mark those things up way more than what they are worth. I'm so thankful that Soph has such sensible taste in clothing. She is always dressed nicely and looks beautiful." Austin said as he wrapped his arm around my waist and pulled me closer to him.

"Dinner is ready, let's eat." My mother said, trying to diffuse the tension in the room. We all walked into the dining room and took a seat at the table. I went to help my mother bring the food to the table. As usual Pamela just sat there like she wasn't raised better. Whatever, I was not going to engage in the sniping banter tonight. I finally have a boyfriend and he makes me very happy.

"May I open the wine and pour?" Austin asked politely. He proceeded to pour wine into our glasses, but Pamela held her hand over her glass.

"I'll just have water, thank you." She said as we stared at her. Pamela always had wine with her dinner. I noticed that she was looking a little green around the gills and then it dawned on me. She's pregnant. Holy shit. She looked at me and her eyes pleaded with me not to say anything. I gave her a small smile and a nod. It was her news, and I would not burst her bubble. "Maybe Sophie should have water too."

"Sophie will have what she likes. If I need to drive her over to pick up her car tomorrow, then I will." Austin said with finality in his voice. Pamela sucked in her breath, and I smiled.

"Thanks babe, I would love another glass." I told him as he winked at me. Dinner was delicious. I was still hungry since I had not had any lunch and I had several glasses of wine. I went to reach for another helping and my mother put her hand on mine.

"Sophie, you want to be able to fit into your bridesmaids' dress in a couple of months. I think you have had enough." My mother said. My face turned red, and I dropped the serving spoon sitting back in my chair. I couldn't believe she was going to embarrass me in front of Austin like that. I was shaking, humiliated and pissed all at the same time. I knew I was going to cry, and I didn't want to do it at the table.

"Please excuse me." I said as I got up to go to the bathroom. I had just passed the dining room door when I heard Austin.

"What is wrong with you. Sophie Ann is a beautiful woman, and she is perfect just the way she is. If she wants two more helpings, then that's what she will have. How dare you insinuate that she is going to be too big to wear a dress in two months. How about buying one that is her size. Which I happen to think looks a hell of a lot better than the stick figure your other daughter is who is picking at her food like she is afraid of it." He stood up and put his napkin on the table. "If you will excuse me, I'm going to go check on my girl."

He turned the corner, and I was standing there with a huge smile on my face and tears in my eyes.

"Baby, are you okay?" he asked me as he pulled me to his chest. He rubbed my back as he held me. "I can't even believe she did that. You are perfect."

"I am now. No one has ever stood up for me like that. I was hungry because I didn't eat lunch. Can we leave?" I asked him. I didn't want to be here anymore.

"Honey, I'm so sorry your mother said that. It was rude and uncalled for." My dad said as he came into the living room. He looked at Austin holding and comforting me and smiled. "Thank you for having her back. You see her the way I see her. She is sweet, smart and beautiful. I don't know what the hell has gotten into Julia, but we will be having a talk later."

"Sir, I want to be respectful of you and your wife. Especially in your own home, but please understand that I will not tolerate anyone disrespecting my woman." Austin said as his hold on me tightened. "I think we have had enough for one evening. I hope that this is not going to be the way Christmas dinner goes because I won't subject her to that kind of verbal and emotional abuse."

"You're right and I apologize for her mother. Again, I will be speaking to her. I look forward to seeing both of you here for Christmas." My dad said as he brushed my cheek with his big hands and kissed the top of my head. "You go take care of my baby, maybe stop and get her a big pepperoni and green olive pizza."

"I'll take care of her; it was nice to meet you. Goodnight." Austin took our coats out of the hall closet and helped me into mine before putting his on. He then led me out to his car and helped me in. We will pick up your car this weekend."

16

Austin 'Gears'

I was furious as we left her parents' house. I could not believe that her own mother would say something so horrible to her. No wonder she was hesitant to eat. What a mind fuck that must be for her. I reached over, took her hand and brought it to my mouth to kiss it.

"Baby, why don't we go get some pizza and go back to my place. You stay with me tonight. We don't have work tomorrow so we can sleep in and just lay around watching Christmas movies all day." I suggested to her. Glancing over I saw her smile at me. It was a small smile but a start. I knew what was said hurt her deeply.

"I need to get some clothes for tomorrow." Sophie said quietly. My girl's spirit was a bit crushed, and I was going to do everything I could to show her how perfect she was.

"My sister is about the same size, and she has plenty of clothes at my place you can borrow." I told her as I called the pizza place and ordered her favorite and a supreme as well. We could eat leftovers for lunch tomorrow. She stared out the window as we went to get the food and then drove back to my house. I parked and went around to open her door. I took the pizza, and we went inside. Flipping on the light I went to get her a T-shirt of mine to wear and a pair of my sister's leggings.

"Here baby, change into this while I get a fire started and we can eat in front of the tv while we watch Christmas movies." I nudged her toward my room, and she disappeared behind my door. I put more wood in the fireplace and got it going. I knew it was a little chilly here. I had unbuttoned my dress shirt and was about to pull it off when Sophie walked in wearing just her bra and panties. They were pale blue lace and fit her curves beautifully. I just stood there staring at her for a few minutes.

"I thought maybe we could work up more of an appetite." She said as she walked towards me. I licked my lips looking at those luscious thighs, wanted to spread her out on the rug and have my dessert now.

"Damn baby, that is some sexy lingerie you have there. I think it needs to come off though." I said as I reached around her and unhooked her bra. She let it fall to the floor and pushed my shirt off my shoulders. I leaned forward and picked her up so I could gently lay her on the floor. I started with her mouth. Kissing her was always a pleasure with those full lips and the sweet sighs she made when I nibbled on that bottom lip. I was already bursting out of my pants. I pulled my shirt off and pulled the belt out of my pants. I used it to restrain her hands above her head. Looping it through the leg of the straight back chair that sat by the fireplace. Then I peeled her lacy underwear down her legs and threw it over my shoulder. She was laying on my fur rug spread out like a feast with the firelight playing over her body. I took off my pants but left my briefs on for now. I wanted to worship her body and show her how special she was. She was all softness and curves. I loved that. Kissing my way down her neck to her collarbone I licked and sucked leaving marks. I wanted everyone to know she was mine. I worked my way down to her breasts taking first the right one into my mouth and sucking it licking at her nipples as they pebbled then switching to the other one. She was moaning and writhing as I licked and kissed my way down her soft abdomen. I don't know why any man would want skin and bones. This softness was made to cushion a man. I took my time in that area so she would understand that I loved every inch of her body just the way it was. Her eyes were on me as I tongued her belly button, and she was flushed. Her legs were wrapped around my lower body, and she was trying to get closer. I chuckled as I lowered myself throwing her legs over my shoulders so I could get to my prize. Her pussy was glistening with moisture and her inner thighs were damp from her arousal. I blew on her and she whimpered, then I licked her front to back delving my tongue into her tight channel. Her thighs were trembling, but I was nowhere near done with her. I gently turned her body and had her on her elbows and knees then I started to lick her taint. She jerked at first then moaned again. My girl liked a little backdoor play. Good to know. I got it nice and wet before going back to her pussy and licking my way up to her clit. I worked a finger in her tight channel and started to fuck her pussy with my finger then added another one. She was still writhing around. I smacked her ass.

"Be still." I said as I bit her ass cheek and she shuddered. I started to work my fingers in and out of her until I could hear the wet sounds of her pussy trying to suck my fingers back in. I reached up with my other hand and rubbed her clit, that was all she needed to start convulsing around my fingers. She was beautiful in her orgasm. I wanted to give her several more before the end of the night. I stood up and stripped off my briefs before getting back on my knees and slamming into her.

"Aust..... oh fuck." She stammered as she was pulsing around me. Apparently, I tipped her back into another orgasm as I started to fuck her hard from behind. She was meeting my thrusts and panting. I reached up and took hold of her breasts, fondling them while I fucked her. I wanted her to know who she belonged to.

"Whose pussy is this? Who do you belong to?" I asked as I continued to fuck her. "Answer me"

"Yours, I belong to you. Harder please. I need to come again." She said huskily as she met me thrust for thrust. I slid out flipped her over and held on leg up pounding into her. I wanted to see her face when we came this time.

"Rub your clit baby, make yourself feel good." I told her as I was getting close. "You are going to come with me. Are you close?"

"Yesssss, almost there….." she stammered as she screamed her orgasm and clinched me pulling mine out with hers. I stayed inside her for a minute catching my breath. I reached up and grabbed a few tissues and gently pulled out of her. I cleaned us up a little before standing up.

"Stay here, I'll be right back." I told her. I went to the bathroom and started a bath. I put a little bubble bath in it that had Epsom salt. Then went to get my girl. She looked well fucked and very satisfied. "Damn your beautiful." I picked her up and carried her to the bathroom. I put her in the tub, lit a few candles and turned off the main light. I then climbed in behind her with a washcloth. She eased back against my chest and sighed. I was in love with this woman. It happened fast. I wanted her the first time I saw her but over the last year I found I liked everything about her, even our banter. I gently ran the washcloth over her body as she snuggled in my arms.

"I love you, Sophie Ann Boyd. I know it's really soon, but I know how I feel" I told her quietly in her ear. She squeezed my hand and turned to look into my eyes.

"I love you too, Austin. We may have only just started dating but we have had chemistry for months and I enjoyed our little arguments too. I always look forward to seeing you at work. Even when I thought I hated you, I wanted you." She said as she turned and climbed into my lap facing me. I'll be damned if I wasn't hard as a rock again. She smiled and raised up seating herself on me. Wrapping her arms around my neck she kissed me and started to raise and lower herself. Taking her pleasure as we made love in the bath. It didn't take long for both of us to finish and when I lifted her off me, I washed us both before getting out and found towels to dry us off.

"Are you hungry, baby?" I asked her as her stomach growled. She blushed and giggled. "I'll take that as a yes. Let's get you dressed and comfy on the couch and I'll warm up our pizza in the oven." I carried her into the bedroom and pulled my shirt over her head, it was long and reached the top of her thighs. I pulled out a pair of my drawstring sweatpants and put them on her. "I like the idea of you in my clothes." I kissed her on the nose, and we went to the living room. I pulled a blanket around her on the couch and put on the Hallmark channel so she could watch Christmas movies. When she was comfy, I heated the oven and put a few slices of each on a sheet pan to warm up. I fixed us both a large glass of ice water so we could rehydrate. When the stove went off, I put our pizza on a couple of plates and carried it to the couch. Settling down behind her we ate and watched 'White Christmas'.

17

Sophie

I woke up the next morning with Austin curled around me. One arm across the pillow over my head and the other tucked under my breasts. I wanted to lay here and enjoy the warm snuggles but my bladder had other ideas. I gently tried to raise his arm and move but he pulled me back down to him.

"Where are you going?" he mumbled in his sleep. "No work, more sleep." I giggled at his response. He was so adorable when he was sleepy.

"I'm just going to the bathroom; I'll be right back. I promise." I leaned over and kissed his scruffy cheek and then went to relieve my bladder. I figured while I was in here, I would brush my hair and my teeth. I looked in the mirror and gasped. I had little bruises all over my lower neck and my collar bone. Oh my God, I was going to have to wear a scarf to the Christmas party or go find a turtleneck dress.

Walking back into the bedroom I crawled back into bed, and he immediately pulled me against his chest. I felt his erection pressing into my ass and I couldn't resist wiggling against him. He groaned and pulled me on top of him.

I was only wearing his shirt and he was nude, so I slid down his dick and rode him to a nice orgasm. After I came, he flipped me over and fucked me hard, reaching around he played with my clit until I came again with him this time. After we went to shower together. Leaving me in the bathroom to dry my hair, Austin went to fix us some coffee. I heard the door and when I came in the living room there was a woman in Austin's arms. I almost lost my shit completely until I saw her lean back and I recognized her from the pictures.

I cleared my throat and the girl jumped back squealing when she saw me. She smacked Austin on the shoulder.

"You have a guest. Why didn't you say something?" She turned to me and walked over and hugged me. "Hi, I'm Dawn. This knucklehead's sister. You must be Sophie."

I instantly relaxed, he had told his sister about me. Austin came over and gave me a kiss and put his arm around me.

"Dawn, this is my Sophie. We were just planning to laze around today but why don't we go out for breakfast." He suggested as he looked at us. I looked down at myself.

"I don't have any clothes to wear. I need to go by my place." I said, looking at Dawn. "Will you excuse us just a second." I dragged him into his bedroom and pointed to my neck. "Oh my God Austin. I look like a leopard."

"Oops, well I'm not really sorry. I wanted everyone to know you are taken." He said as he kissed me again. I swear he can get his way just by doing this. I lose brain cells when he kisses me. "I told you Dawn has some clothes you can borrow."

Just then I heard a knock on the bedroom door. "Sophie, I have a turtleneck and some jeans laid out for you to borrow along with some panties I have never worn. I'm going to go see Undertaker and Annie's baby. I'll meet you at the diner."

We heard the front door shut and looked at each other and laughed. Clearly, she noticed my issue as well. I shook my head and went to the living area to grab the clothes she laid out for me. I slipped on the jeans, some socks and the sweater which thankfully covered his marks. I had worn boots over here, so they looked fine with the jeans. I wasn't going to be wearing makeup because I didn't have any with me. I watched Austin pull on his boots and grab our jackets as we headed out the door. We saw Dawn pulling away from the front of Undertakers' place a few minutes later.

"I had no idea she was coming home. She said she couldn't make it." He said sounding apologetic. I squeezed his hand.

"Don't be silly, I'm glad your sister is able to spend Christmas with us. If you want to ditch my parent's dinner, I can go alone and then meet you here after." I told him. He pulled up to the diner and got out. After opening my door, he pressed me against the car.

"No way in hell am I letting you go alone. Your father is the only one in that house that seems to love you for who you are, but he didn't stand up for you. I will be there. Dawn wants to hang out with her best friend anyway. Tessa is a nurse, and she will be working so Dawn will take her dinner. She will meet us for the clubhouse meal later in the evening." He stated firmly and kissed me again. Then took my hand and led me into the diner. When we walked in, we spotted a couple of guys in the back. "Let's go introduce you to a couple of my friends."

They stood up and introduced themselves to me. First was Fury who was very handsome in a scary kind of way. He didn't smile much but the one smile he gave me would have been a panty dropper if I wasn't totally in love with the guy next to me. Next was Rider, he was a jovial guy who seemed to always have jokes. Last was Doc, he was movie star handsome with beautiful curly thick hair and a killer smile. He was staring at Dawn. She had come in behind us. The guys sat back down, and we went to sit with Dawn when my phone rang. I looked down and saw it was Cara.

"Babe, I need to take this, it's my best friend and I haven't talked to her in a couple of days." I told him as I kissed his cheek and walked out front for a minute.

"Hey girl, everything okay?" I asked her, I knew she was likely mad because I had not had a chance to catch her up."

"Yes, except that I haven't heard from you in three days. What the hell Sophie?" Cara said sounding hurt. "Are we still on for Christmas breakfast?

"Of course, same place, same time as every year." I told her, reminding me I needed to get my car. "I have so much to tell you."

"Good I miss you and I need the deets on that guy from work." she said in a curious voice. "You were going out with him and then I didn't hear much after that."

"That is going really great, I am actually at breakfast with him and his sister, so I need to go back in. Let me know if you need help at the shelter later." I told her and she agreed. We hung up and I went back inside. "Have you guys ordered yet?"

"No baby, we were waiting for you. What would you like?" He asked, and I swooned what a gentleman. "I'll have the breakfast special, eggs scrambled." The waitress took our orders and left us to chat.

"I'm so sorry I barged in on you two this morning." Dawn said blushing. "I was excited to finish my dissertation early and I wanted to surprise Gearhead here."

I giggled at the nickname seeing him blush. "Don't be silly, it's your home. I'm glad to get to meet you."

We ate breakfast and talked for a bit, getting to know each other. I noticed it was getting close to eleven.

"We need to go get my car and you two should totally catch up." I said as I put my napkin on my plate. Austin got up and dropped a fifty-dollar bill on the table. He put his arm around us both as we walked outside.

"I'm going to go see Tessa, do you two want to do dinner tonight?" she asked with a smile. I was thrilled that she seemed to like me, so I agreed as long as he was okay with it. I did let him know that I needed to go home tonight. I had some shopping to do, and I needed to get ready for our party at home. We watched Dawn walk across the street to the clinic and we headed to my parents' to get my car.

18

Austin 'Gears'

I loved my sister, but I had been looking forward to spending the day secluded with my girl. Sophie took it all in stride though. She and Dawn hit it off right away. I was relieved that the two women who mean the most to me got along.

I was super proud of her for finishing what she needed to do to be here. We picked up Sophie's car and I kissed her, telling her I would see her at my place around five. I had nothing else to do until later, so I decided to go shopping for a gift for Sophie. I drove past the jewelry store and turned back around. I parked and walked inside. I must be crazy we haven't been together that long. The thing is I knew she was the one. I wanted to be with her. The clerk walked over to greet me, and I told him what I was looking for. I had seen her wear mostly yellow gold, and all her jewelry was understated. I knew that a simple solitaire was the way to go. I spotted a princess cut diamond on a thick yellow gold band. I realized I didn't know what size ring she wore. I would just go with the stock size, and we could have it adjusted if need be. I looked around for a gift for Dawn. She would be graduating in a few months, so I decided on a nice watch. I found a white gold Bulova watch that she would love. I paid for both and had them wrapped up. Taking the bag out to the car I decided to head home and figure out dinner.

A few hours later Dawn came in to shower and change. At five Sophie knocked on the door. She had a pass at the gate to let her in whenever. Those were few and far between. She looked lovely, I kissed her and told her to take a seat while I fixed her a glass of wine.

Dinner went well, we all enjoyed a pot of chicken and dumplings. After dinner Dawn said she was going to go stay at Tessa's place. I followed Sophie home and ended up staying with her. The Christmas party went off without a hitch. Brittni didn't even show up for it. Thank goodness.

Club business was going well. Fang was running Trixie's, and the garage was doing great. Things were good. Annie was indeed expecting again to which we all took great joy in teasing Undertaker about his magic sperm.

It was two days before Christmas, and I was supposed to be meeting Sophie at her place for dinner and I would stay with her. We had not spent a night apart in the last week. I had my overnight bag in my car and had picked up some flowers for her. When I arrived at her place, I saw the lights all off, her car was in its spot. I tried to call her, but I got no answer. Something was wrong. She had given me the code to get in, so I went and checked her place. There had been a struggle and there was some blood on the floor by the door. Her purse was lying on the table. Her phone was lying on the floor by the coffee table. My heart was in my throat. I pulled my phone out and called Fury, Rider and Axle. I didn't want to bother Hawk he was busy with Bethann and her nephews. I picked it up and saw that she had started to type a name. Looks like it was knocked out of her hand before she could finish.

"Brit....." was all that I saw. I knew immediately that bitch Brittni was behind this. She must have figured out that she was busted and going to be fired. That was why she didn't show up at the party. I messaged the guys and told them I was going to have to get into the system at work and get her personnel file so I could get her address. I hoped she didn't take her anywhere else. Damn, I had to find my girl. We didn't hurt women, so I called the local police and had them come check out the apartment. After they arrived, I had Rider stay with them while Axle and Fury went with me. We got the address and went to find Sophie. I wasn't about to wait for the cops to decide they had a lead. I would get Sophie home safe, and we would turn Brittni in for kidnapping and assault.

19

Sophie

I walked into my apartment and knew something was off. All the lights were off. I always leave a lamp on and the light over the stove on. My door was unlocked and not even really closed. I started to turn around when I felt a gun pressed to my side. I looked over and saw Brittni standing there looking all crazy.

"You bitch, you just had to start dating the one guy I always liked. What does he even see in you? I don't understand your short, fat and you dress like an old lady. I tried to get you fired but it was obvious that he was on to me. This is all your fault. I wanted a way out of the trailer park, and he was going to be it. I know he would have asked me out eventually if you had not thrown yourself at him." She kept shoving me toward the couch. She pushed me down and started ranting again. I was terrified. This woman had flipped her lid. I knew she was a bit self-centered, but I didn't realize she was completely delusional and unhinged. I still had an hour before Austin got here for dinner. I was pretty sure she was going to try to get me out of here. I pulled out my phone carefully and started to type her name in before she saw me and knocked the phone out of my hand. Then she slapped me with the gun busting my lip. Shoving the gun under my chin, she walked me out to her car, opened her trunk and pushed me in. My head was spinning, and I was going to be sick. I don't know what she had planned for me, but I know it wasn't good. I tried to kick the lights out of the back of the car so I could try to get someone's attention. Unfortunately, this was a really small town and there was hardly anyone on the back road this time of day. I stuck my arm out cutting it on the glass, but I kept trying to wave and get attention. We turned and stopped suddenly. I pulled my arm back inside the car and tried to wrap my jacket around the cut.

The truck popped open, and she was enraged. "You stupid cunt, you busted my damn lights out. Do you have any idea how much that will cost for me to have fixed?" She shot me in the shoulder, and I screamed. Suddenly I saw her get jerked away from me and the gun knocked out of her hand. Austin looked inside and saw me. He looked absolutely murderous.

"Baby, oh my God, where are you hurt. Did that bitch shoot you?" he reached inside and gently pulled me out. Yelling for Rider to have Doc meet us at the clinic. "Damn, I'm so sorry."

"I love you Austin, not your fault. I'm gonna be sick." I leaned over and threw up. I couldn't stop vomiting. I was fading in and out. Next thing I knew I was in a cold room, and I saw Doc, then I was out again.

I woke up in a scratchy bed with an annoying beeping noise and my shoulder hurt so bad. My head was pounding, and I was so thirsty. I opened my eyes and saw Austin's head laying on his arms on the bed. He looked like he had slept there all night.

"Austin, honey." I tried to say with a scratchy voice. He jerked awake and saw me. Immediately he put his arms around me gently and kissed my lips, my cheeks, my eyes. He looked so distraught, if I had any doubts about his feelings for me, I didn't anymore.

"I'm so sorry she hurt you. I won't ever let anyone hurt you again. I love you so much." He said as I pointed to my throat. "Oh, your thirsty, I'll get you some water. Doc said the intubation would make your throat a little sore. They got the bullet out and you have a mild concussion, they also stitched up your arm where you cut it sticking it out of the light slot."

I drank some of the water slowly and then he put the cup down. Doc walked into the room and smiled; he really was a beautiful man.

"Hey, you don't need to be thinking any other man is beautiful." Austin grumbled as I blushed. Doc just chuckled and winked at me.

"Oh good, my patient is awake. You gave us quite a scare little lady. This guy had not left your side except for surgery, and I thought we were going to have to restrain him to keep him out of the OR. We had to give you a couple of units of blood. You are going to have to stay here for another twenty-four hours. If you're good, I'll release you Christmas afternoon. We will be here playing Santa that morning and then I'll do release papers and get you out of here." He looked at Austin and motioned him to the door, said something and then closed the door behind him.

"Your parents are in the waiting room. Doc told the hospital staff that I was your fiance`. I wanted to do this differently but I'm not waiting another minute. Sophie Ann Boyd, you have had my attention since the moment I saw you and you have claimed my heart along the way. I want to marry you, give you babies and grow old with you. Will you do me the honor of being my wife?" I stared at him for a minute and then saw he had a ring in his hand.

"Yes, I would love to be your wife. I don't want a long engagement or a big wedding. Just something small with our close friends and family." I told him as he put the ring on my finger and kissed my hand holding it to his face.

"Did I just hear my baby is engaged?" my dad said as he came into the room. He shook Austin's hand and winked at him. "Congratulations, welcome to the family son."

My mother peaked around the corner. She looked sad and embarrassed. I had not spoken to her since the awful dinner. I wasn't sure I wanted to talk to her now but I would give her a chance.

"Can I come in for a minute?" she asked, looking at the two of us. "Please, I want to apologize. I don't know what got into me and I'm so sorry that I ever made you feel anything but beautiful. I love you so much. Your sister will be here in the morning she is working late so she can come for Christmas and be off a few days to help you."

"I love you too Mom. You really hurt me about the food and my weight. You know I have always struggled with it. I don't have yours or Pamela's metabolism. I can't help it." Austin growled at what I said.

"You are perfect, I told you I don't want a stick." he said firmly. "Your parents and I had a long talk while you were in surgery. They have been invited along with your sister, her fiance` and your friend Cara to have dinner at the clubhouse with us. They know I'm part of the Rippers' MC and accept that we are also your family and will always have your back."

"The doctor said you could go home tomorrow afternoon, Austin informed us that home was his house and he has already had his sister and the guys move your stuff over." My mom said. I looked at Austin and he looked a little sheepish.

"I may have jumped the gun; I was anxious to be sure you were taken care of and safe." He said holding my hand. I smiled and shook my head a little. Bad idea, the movement hurt. "Does your head hurt baby?"

"Yes, the light and too much conversation." I told him. He started to move away but I held onto his hand. "Mom, will you find the doctor and let him know I need some pain meds, and then can you guys go home, and I'll see you tomorrow. I need more sleep."

"Sure honey. We will see you tomorrow. Austin, thank you for finding and saving our baby girl." My mother hugged him and then my dad led her out of the room.

"Now can you please get up here with me and hold me. You can lay on my right side since my injured arm and IV are on the left." I asked him. He kissed me and gently moved the covers, and I slid over just a bit so he would fit then curled into him. He covered us up. "I'm so tired, I love you and yes I'm happy to move in with you."

Doc came in and administered some pain medicine in my IV, he didn't make any comments about Austin being in bed with me.

20

Austin 'Gears'

Christmas Day was different this year. I was more excited about it and looking forward to the new year. I left Sophie sleeping this morning with a note on the side table. She knew I had to go help get the gifts to the hospital and down to the children's ward this morning. Undertaker would be arriving on his sleigh with all the toys. It was an MC tradition from back when I was little. We helped get everything inside, he made a big deal of carrying the bag down the ward. The kids who were mobile were seated in the waiting room by the Christmas tree. The children who couldn't get out of bed were taken care of first. We went around, gave them their gifts and took pictures of them with Santa and then gathered in the waiting room to pass out gifts and read the Christmas Story. About eleven I saw Doc come in with his white coat on and his festive tie, he always wore a Santa hat on Christmas. He only worked a half day unless there was an emergency. He nodded to me, and I followed him to Sophie's room. She was sitting up dressed and ready to go. Her friend Cara was there waiting with her. She smiled when she saw me and nudged Sophie, who was talking to her mom on the phone. She finished her call and held out her arms to me.

This woman was going to be my wife. If I had my way it would be a New Years Eve wedding. I wanted to start the year with her as Mrs. Sophie Wilson. I wrapped her in my arms and kissed her.

"Merry Christmas my love. Doc said he has already had you sign the papers let's get you out of here." I told her as I picked her up and placed her in the wheelchair. She wrinkled her cute little nose, but Doc told her it was policy, so she put up with it. "You look beautiful."

"Thanks, Cara brought me something to wear. I know that I'll be parking it on the couch at the clubhouse until dinner is served, she is going to keep me company. My parents will be there about half an hour before dinner. Mom is bringing the sweet potato casserole I wanted to bring. Pamela and James will be there in time for dinner. Pammy called an apologized." She was beautiful but I could tell that just getting dressed took a lot out of her. I was going to try and have her take a nap on the couch while dinner was being made.

"The ring is beautiful Austin, congratulations on winning her heart. You better guard it with your life or I'll be coming after you." Cara said with a serious look on her face but a twinkle in her eyes. She winked at me.

We arrived at the clubhouse and there was sign up that said, "Welcome home Sophie." My girl started to cry. I rubbed her back and then settled into a recliner with her in my arms. I pulled a blanket around us and held her while she fell asleep. The guys all smiled as they passed us. I saw Hawk come in with Bethann and her nephews. He was holding a large dish in one hand and Joshua in the other. They had really taken to him; he got the boys settled in a corner in front of the tv. He put on the Christmas parade for them to watch and Dawn went to sit on the floor with them. People started coming in dropping off dishes.

Lillian was leading the brigade and bossing everyone in the kitchen. She made sure the tables were decorated and set. The drink table and food tables were prepped with warmers. Everything smelled delicious. I woke Sophie up so I could carry her to the table for dinner. As we all gathered around the table, I thought about how blessed I was to have this huge family and that now I had more.

Doc offered the prayer, and we all gave thanks. Before we started to eat Sophie looked at me and smiled really big.

"Austin 'Gears' Wilson, I love you so much. Thank you for being my Christmas boyfriend and my forever love. Merry Christmas!

The End.

Made in United States
Troutdale, OR
05/17/2024

19937030R00066